Ex's and Oh's

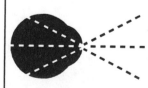

This Large Print Book carries the
Seal of Approval of N.A.V.H.

EX'S AND OH'S

SANDRA STEFFEN

THORNDIKE PRESS
An imprint of Thomson Gale, a part of The Thomson Corporation

THOMSON
™
GALE

Detroit • New York • San Francisco • New Haven, Conn. • Waterville, Maine • London • Munich

THOMSON

TM

GALE

LIBRARY OF CONGRESS CATALOGING-IN-PUBLICATION DATA

Steffen, Sandra.
    Ex's and oh's / by Sandra Steffen.
        p. cm. — (Thorndike Press large print Americana)
    ISBN 0-7862-8959-7 (alk. paper)
        1. Single women — Fiction. 2. Pregnant women — Fiction. 3. Large type books. I. Title.
    PS3619.T447E9 2006
    813'.54—dc22
                                                                    2006018600

Published in 2006 by arrangement with Harlequin Books S.A.

Printed in the United States of America on permanent paper
10 9 8 7 6 5 4 3 2 1

For my uncle, Lyle Steffen, who tells the best stories about the good old days.

And for the nurses, aides, therapists and all the staff who care for the residents at Hazel Findlay Country Manor with kindness, compassion and dignity.

ACKNOWLEDGMENTS

A special thank-you to Jennifer Green, a brilliant young attorney whose knowledge of the law and its terminology aided me so much in my creation of Caroline Moore in this story. And I must commend Susan Meeder for her descriptions and firsthand knowledge of Charlevoix, Michigan. And always, thank you, Linda Thelen, fellow writer and brainstormer extraordinaire. A heartfelt thanks to my busy and talented editor, Melissa Jeglinski, and also to Tara Gavin, editorial director. Hats off to both of you for giving me the opportunity to tell my poignant stories.

CHAPTER 1

If one more person asked Caroline Moore if she was all right, she was going to explode. And Caroline never exploded. She breathed deeply. She meditated. She looked beyond any given situation, considering every possible angle. But she didn't explode.

Today was different. Today, she'd buried her grandfather. And no, she wasn't all right. All right wasn't even close.

Seeing the last of the neighbors to the door, she closed her eyes, her hand going automatically to her throat. The collar of her silk blouse was open, her necklace a fine gold chain from which hung a delicate charm that had been her mother's. There was nothing physically restrictive, yet she felt a constraint so tight it was difficult to breathe.

"Are you all right, Caroline?" Steven Phillips asked.

She forced a deep breath, tamped down

an inner explosion and did her best to pull herself together. A fellow attorney, Steven was widely known for his litigation expertise. She'd been seeing him since his divorce became final a year ago. He'd been preoccupied lately. But then, so had she.

She joined him at the French doors, their shoulders close but not quite touching. Neither seemed to have any desire to move closer.

"It's been a long few days for you," he said.

Forty-two years old, Steven was of average height and build. The silver in his hair gave him a wizened look clients trusted. Looking at him, it occurred to her that he had something on his mind. That made two of them. "There's something I need to talk to you about, Steven."

One of the reasons he won so many lawsuits for his clients was that he was good at bluffing. He wasn't just good at it; he was stupendous at it, which made whatever she glimpsed in his eyes more alarming. Instinctively, she proceeded with caution. "Can you come to dinner at my apartment downtown tomorrow evening?"

"I can't make it tomorrow night, Caroline."

Normally, he was a talker. She found it

strange that he didn't elaborate. Fighting a bout of queasiness, she said, "Perhaps this shouldn't wait until tomorrow anyway."

He glanced sharply at her. "I was going to tell you."

He was going to tell *her?* What was he talking about? Luckily, she was good at bluffing, too. "When?" she asked. "When were you planning to tell me?"

A muscle worked in his jaw, and something clicked in her brain. She'd handled enough divorce cases to recognize someone guilty of cheating. "God, Steven."

"It's not like that." There was nothing quite like a lawyer jumping to his own defense. "Brenda and I have been talking, and we've come to realize the divorce was a mistake."

A mistake? That was a good one. "The woman you're seeing behind my back is your *ex-wife?*"

"She's the mother of my children. Believe me, this is not sordid."

The floor pitched. Regaining her equilibrium, she said, "Then you haven't been sleeping with both of us?"

His mouth thinned and his expression hardened. "I know this is a shock, but frankly, I'm a little surprised you're upset."

Trying to think, Caroline fingered the

charm on her necklace. Her life was falling apart around her, but this wasn't the surprise she'd had in mind.

"I'm sorry," Steven said. "I know this is a difficult time for you. That's why we didn't want to tell you until you'd had a chance to —"

We?

"Brenda knows about me? About us?"

"I didn't want to begin our trial reconciliation with a lie between us. I've never seen my boys this happy. Think about them."

He wanted her to think about his children. That was priceless.

"They've been in counseling since the divorce. Brenda and I have been worried about them. You and I have talked about that."

A few months earlier, Caroline had spent an afternoon at the aquarium with Steven's sons. The outing had been awkward and difficult. Caroline didn't pretend to know much about children, but the boys' dislike for her had been painfully obvious.

"I'm sorry about your grandfather. I know how you felt about Henry. In fact, I've always gotten the impression he was the only man you needed in your life."

She felt hollow, empty and bereft. She wanted to tell him she had needs, too, but her pride kept her still. "I think you should go, Steven."

She hated him for looking relieved.

At the door he said, "It's not as if you've ever mentioned the future, let alone one that included marriage or a family."

It was difficult to know whether to laugh or cry.

He was watching her, his head turned at an unnatural angle, accentuating his long neck and prominent Adam's apple. "I've fallen in love with my ex-wife all over again. Haven't you ever been in love?"

He let himself out without waiting for her answer.

Caroline couldn't seem to stop shaking. She closed the French doors, then stared through the wavy glass, shivering. Her grandfather's favorite mesh patio furniture faced Lake Michigan, which today was as gray as the May sky. How many times had she found him sitting there, quietly looking out across the vast water?

He'd been her only family since her parents' deaths when she was eight. It couldn't have been easy for him, and yet he'd taken her in and made a home for her. He'd devoted his life to raising her.

She shivered again. For some reason, Steven's question about being in love really

13

bothered her. She'd thought she was in love once or twice a long time ago, but the sentiment had faded. It was a well-known fact that women had to work twice as hard as men in this field. She'd worked three times as hard. She'd set goals and systematically met each one. In doing so, she'd made sacrifices along the way. And no, she'd never been truly in love. Until recently, that hadn't felt like a tragedy. But Caroline had bigger problems. One big problem, to be exact.

Maria Gonzales, her grandfather's housekeeper, was washing dishes when Caroline entered the kitchen a few minutes later.

"Could you use some help?" Caroline asked.

"I could use some company," Maria answered. "Sit. I don't know how you walk in those shoes."

Caroline didn't trust herself to smile, so she did as Maria said, lowering to the chair where she'd eaten breakfast every morning during her formative years. Leaning back, she slid her feet out of her Manolo Blahniks. The shoes had been a gift to herself after she won the Hiller-Dalton case last month. Once, a reporter had called her penchant for buying expensive, imported shoes a fetish. Caroline hadn't addressed the reporter's statement, for doing so would have lent it credence, which would have been stupid. And Caroline had never been stupid.

Until recently, that is.

"Try not to think," Maria said, drying a platter. "It will all work out. You'll see. I told my Carmen the same thing this morning. She's eighteen now, and a worrier like her father."

Caroline looked at the family photograph Maria kept on the windowsill. Maria and her husband Miguel had three children: Carmen, Dominic and the baby. He must be four now. His name escaped Caroline. Maria had come to work for Henry O'Shaughnessy the same year Caroline left to study law at Columbia University in New York. She'd always treated Caroline well, and vice versa, and yet in all the years they'd known each other and all the times they'd spoken, most of their conversations had been about Caroline's grandfather or the weather or the news. Now she regretted that they'd never shared more personal information.

"Am I coldhearted, Maria?"

Maria took so long considering the question that Caroline braced herself for an unpleasant truth.

15

Finally, Maria said, "You're busy, but you're not cold. You're like your shoes. Beautiful, supple, exquisitely crafted, but out of the average person's league."

The description made Caroline sigh.

In so many ways, Caroline and Maria were opposites. Their common link had been their mutual love for Henry O'Shaughnessy. Caroline's grandfather had been stubborn and well-spoken, kind and opinionated until he'd died suddenly of a heart attack four days ago. There was no question that he'd loved them, too. His last will and testament had already been read, Maria's dedication rewarded handsomely. She'd agreed to stay on until Caroline decided what to do with the beautiful old house. Although not a decadent amount, the inheritance gave Maria options she hadn't expected. Caroline knew the other woman would have managed without the monetary gift, for she was one of those women who knew how to be happy regardless of her situation.

Caroline envied her that.

"How old are you, Maria?"

Looking surprised by the question, she said, "I'm thirty-eight. Antonio thinks his mother is old."

Antonio. The baby's name was Antonio. But Maria wasn't old. She was five years younger than Caroline. "Look at all you have."

Laying a hand over Caroline's, Maria said, "You're just a late bloomer. Now you will catch up. There's nothing like having a baby. You'll see."

Caroline's mouth dropped open. She hadn't told a soul about this. She'd thrown the home pregnancy kit in the trash downtown. Until this week, she'd had no morning sickness, and that she'd attributed to shock and sadness. According to her calculations, she was only two-and-a-half months along. "How did you know?"

"When you've been there three times," Maria said sagely, "you recognize the signs. Plus, it's been several months since anything has been moved on the middle shelf in the bathroom you use when you stay here. Are you hoping for a boy or a girl?"

Until that moment, Caroline hadn't allowed herself to think in those terms. When she was late the first month, she'd blamed it on stress. Two weeks later she'd researched early menopause on the Internet. By the second month she'd decided it was most likely cancer. She couldn't be pregnant. She was on the pill. Besides, single, forty-three-year-old crackerjack attorneys who worked their butts off to make partner did not have surprise pregnancies.

"What did Señor Phillips say?"

"He's going back to his ex-wife and their two kids."

"But how — what about — you didn't tell him?"

Shaking her head, Caroline watched for Maria's reaction.

Maria took the information in stride the way she took everything in stride. She took life exactly as it was. She didn't try to manipulate it, change it or get around it.

Caroline envied her that, as well.

"Now," Maria said, "if you're lucky, the baby won't have a skinny neck and big Adam's apple. Just to be safe, let's hope it's a girl."

Why on earth that struck Caroline funny, she didn't know. A tight little laugh squeezed out of her. Half hiccup, half croak, another followed, and another, and another. Maria joined her. Soon, they were both laughing uncontrollably. Maria was clutching her middle and slapping at Caroline to stop, and Caroline was wiping tears.

Without warning, the sounds no longer came from Caroline's belly, but from her chest, turning mournful, sorrowful. Tears of laughter had fallen freely. These tears burned her eyes, leaving hot trails down her face. She cried and cried, for her grandfather, for her parents whom she'd lost so long ago, and for her life that was suddenly out of control.

Her eyes wet, too, Maria placed a box of tissues on Caroline's lap. Standing beside her, she held Caroline's face to her chest, rocking her as she would one of her children. By the time the episode finally passed, Caroline felt depleted, wretched, spent.

"Do you want me to stay for a while?" Maria asked after Caroline had blown her nose and dried her eyes.

Caroline appreciated the offer and told Maria so. "Your family is waiting for you at home."

Removing her apron and hanging it on a hook inside the basement door, Maria said, "Now you'll have a family, too."

Maria hadn't so much as considered the possibility that Caroline might choose one of her other options. Perhaps it was Maria's upbringing. Or perhaps she sensed just how much Caroline wanted this child.

She wondered if she was the only one who thought it was ironic that her closest confidante was the family housekeeper. And until today, Caroline hadn't even known the name of Maria's youngest child.

"Something is seriously wrong with me

and with my life, Maria."

"Sometimes things must go wrong before you know what you need to fix. Now you know."

With that enormous vote of confidence, Maria left. It was several minutes before Caroline realized something was different.

She could breathe.

CHAPTER 2

On the Saturday following her grandfather's funeral, Caroline let herself into his stately house in Lake Forest. She'd come for the same reason she'd done it yesterday and the day before. She needed to prove he was truly gone.

She wandered through each room, touching the book still open to the last page he'd read, breathing in the scent of Old Spice aftershave on the shirt hanging neatly over his bedside chair. Caroline was going to have to decide what to do with the house. More importantly, she needed to decide what to do about her life. She'd managed on her own for years and suddenly she couldn't seem to make a decision.

For some reason, she opened the attic door and went up. At the top of the stairs she pulled the string attached to a bare bulb. Dust particles floated on slats of sunlight slanting through the louvered shutters at the end of the long narrow room. Old sofas and chairs crouched beneath canvas tarps and muslin sheets. Antique trunks, dressers, chests, and all those useless items her grandfather couldn't part with were stacked nearly to the sloped ceiling.

Caroline would never forget the first time she'd seen this room. Her grandfather had just collected her from a neighbor in Boston after her parents' plane went down. He'd driven all day and all night to bring her to his home in this historical district north of Chicago. Although she'd visited Lake Forest often prior to that day, it was different without her mom and dad. Everything was different without them.

Scared and alone, she'd awakened the first night in her unfamiliar bed. With a whimper, she'd slipped out of the high four-poster. The lamp was on in her grandfather's study, but the room was empty. A door hung open at the end of the hall. Following a dim light, she'd crept to the top of the attic stairs.

She'd found her grandfather sitting at a desk beneath the window, an album of some sort open on his lap. With his head bowed, his face downturned, he could have been an old oil painting. Hearing her approach, he'd looked straight at her. So heavy was his sigh, it might have weighed a hundred pounds. It seemed to Caroline that neither of them moved for a very long time. All the while, something unspoken and sorrowful passed between their gazes.

He finally closed the album and placed it on the desk. He removed his wire-rimmed glasses. Folding them painstakingly, he tucked them into his chest pocket. He'd done it exactly that way until the day he died, but that night, it was new to her, and she'd put it to memory.

Holding out his hand, his voice had been deep and thick with emotion as he said, "Come, child."

She couldn't have flown to him, but it had felt that way to her as she'd darted barefoot across the dusty plank floor and scrambled onto his lap. Closing her eyes, she'd burrowed into him. He didn't smell flowery like her mother and he wasn't broad and solid like her father. She was eight and he seemed ancient, but there was strength in his hands, patience in his eyes and kindness in his voice. And although she'd somehow known that her life would never be the same again, she knew she was safe here. She was home.

All these years later, the house in Lake Forest was empty without him. It was hers now. Should she live here with her baby? Or would it be better to start over someplace brand-new?

She lowered carefully into the old desk chair. A thick layer of dust covered every surface of the desk. Each cubby still held some item her grandfather had once used. There were yellowed envelopes, old ledgers, handwritten receipts and postage stamps from the 1940s. He'd been an attorney, and a fastidious one.

In the drawers, she found leather binders, old books and rusty paper clips. One drawer contained the album her grandfather had been looking at that night so long ago. Beneath it was a metal box. Prying off the rusted lid, she removed several items. The first was a black-and-white photograph. It had been taken at too great a distance to tell who the young woman and two men were. The lighthouse in the background didn't look familiar, either. Laying the photograph aside with the album, she returned to the box. Beneath pressed wildflowers, nearly powdery now, she found a sheet of yellowed paper, folded in half, an old skeleton key and a pair of wire-rimmed glasses with Henry O'Shaughnessy engraved on one bow.

She unfolded the sheet of fine stationery, the name Anna O'Shaughnessy professionally printed across the top. It was dated

1943, and it appeared to have been written by Caroline's grandmother.

This morning, Henry and I returned to the lighthouse in Harbor Woods. As I looked across the vast waters of Lake Michigan, I pictured the waves of an ocean instead, and I wondered if the sun was warming Karl's shoulders and curly red hair. I hate this war, and every day I pray for his safety. It does no good to think about what might have been, and yet I cannot help it sometimes. I haven't heard from Karl since I wrote to tell him of my marriage to Henry. I wonder if he burned that letter or kept it to read again. It pains me to think of him hurting. I hope that one day he'll come to understand that I'm trying to do what's best.

Memories of last summer weigh on my heart and on my mind, memories of Karl Peterson, of the love we shared and the life we created. Perhaps that is why I took the diary along today. It has no place in my life now, and yet I couldn't bring myself to destroy it. Doing so would be like destroying the love I gave, the love I received. The diary belongs there, with my past, a written legacy of the summer of my seventeenth year.

Henry was waiting for me as I pulled the heavy cottage door closed. Together, we walked to the truck filled with our belongings. He held the baby while I got in, then smiled down at her, the seed planted by one man, to be raised by another. Henry has never questioned my feelings, nor I his. He loves Elsa, and it doesn't matter to him that her baby-fine hair is coming in red. I don't know what I would have done without him these past eight months.

I am lucky to have been loved by two good men. I wonder if they are as lucky to have been loved by me.

Caroline stared at the delicate handwriting for a long time, her fingertips going to the fine gold chain around her neck. Elsa was Caroline's mother's name.

She found herself studying the black-and-white photograph again. The girl must have been her grandmother, who'd died of pneumonia when Caroline's mother was five. In his younger days, Henry O'Shaughnessy's hair had been pitch-black. The man on Anna's right was most likely him. The other man's hair was lighter and wavy, his head tilted slightly, his stance more cocksure. Karl Peterson?

The seed planted by one man to be raised by another.

Caroline's mother hadn't been Henry's biological child? He must have known. Of course he'd known. And yet he'd never told her.

He was telling her now. It was almost as if she could hear him say there was more to the story. The question was, what was she supposed to do about it?

Caroline was staring into space when a sharp rap sounded on her office door.

"May I come in?" Sheila Ross asked.

Sheila was already in, but Caroline let it go. "Of course. How are you?"

Sheila Ross had become a full partner in the firm when it was almost unheard-of for a woman to do so. Sixty now, she'd married young, divorced shortly thereafter, then never repeated the mistake. She'd given Caroline advice over the years, but for the most part, she'd been dangled like a carrot in front of Caroline's nose. If Caroline worked hard enough, was savvy enough, smart enough, won enough cases, high-profile and otherwise, if she sat on the right committees and attended the right parties, luncheons and fund-raisers, she, too, *might* make full partner one day.

"I'm fine," Sheila said, pulling out a chair. "The question is, how are you?" Petite and trim, she kept her hair a natural-looking shade of light brown. She had good taste in shoes, wore fabulous suits, liked expensive jewelry and fine wine and had small, razor-sharp eyes.

"I'm fine, thank you," Caroline said. "That's two fines and no court costs."

It was a lawyer joke. Sheila didn't pretend to smile. Caroline tried to recall if she'd ever heard the woman laugh or smile and mean it.

"Are you sure you're all right?" Sheila asked.

Caroline wasn't surprised by this visit. She'd passed a very difficult case to Sid Johnson at this morning's staff meeting, then had nearly fallen asleep after lunch. The partners were worried her grief was turning into depression. She *was* grieving, but she wasn't depressed, per se. She had a lot on her mind. She was nearly three-and-a-half months along. She wouldn't be able to keep her pregnancy a secret much longer.

"Perhaps it would help to talk about it," Sheila said.

Caroline almost said, *To you? Surely you're kidding.*

She'd spotted last week, and had rushed

to her doctor, who'd reassured her that light spotting wasn't uncommon during the first trimester. Just to be on the safe side, she'd prescribed bed rest for a few days, and had advised Caroline not to overdo. Caroline had spent the time in bed thinking about her mother, and remembering all the times she'd needed her over the years. Caroline couldn't imagine telling Sheila *that* any more than she could imagine confiding how terrified she'd been of losing the baby.

"I heard Steven Phillips has reconciled with his ex-wife."

"I heard that, too," Caroline said, meeting the other woman's gaze.

"And you're not upset about it?"

"Believe me, he was more attractive and far more interesting over legal briefs and take-out Chinese."

Silently declaring a tie in the ensuing stare-down, Sheila chose a different tack. "You know how sorry everyone here with Hilliard, Ross and Whitley was, is, about your loss."

"I appreciate that, Sheila."

"It's been a month, Caroline. I know how you felt about Henry. He was a dear old man. He lived a good, long life. Some people would argue that it's less traumatic to lose someone who's old. Whether it is or not is immaterial. The important thing is that you don't allow mourning to interfere with your goals."

Caroline had to fight valiantly not to yawn, which earned her a warning thinly disguised as a lecture on the importance of compartmentalizing, particularly for "women like them."

"Women like us?" Caroline asked.

"Yes. Women who are not only smarter than most men, but who are smarter than most women."

Caroline wondered what was so wonderful about being smart. What did Sheila have to show for her intellect, for all her hard work, her cunning, her razor-sharp mind? Invitations to the governor's ball? A reputation for being as approachable as a porcupine? When all was said and done, would anyone ever discover a written entry from someone who'd ached for her? Would anyone care, truly care, when Sheila Ross died?

It seemed to Caroline that all the rest was immaterial.

She'd taken a long, hard look at her life and found it sadly lacking. It wasn't as if she expected to find true love, whatever that was. She had no brothers or sisters. But there might be other relatives. What about friends? Other than Maria, Caroline's

30

friends were more like acquaintances. Shouldn't there be a stronger connection to the people in her life?

What about her baby, and motherhood?

Questions plagued her. She didn't have a clue whether she had what it took to be a good friend or a good mother, but she wanted to try. She hadn't a clue how to define herself anymore. She knew she no longer wanted to be like Sheila Ross. And as Sheila left her office, Caroline was pretty sure the other woman knew it.

Caroline sat in silence for several minutes after the door closed. There were files to open, case profiles to study and evaluate, laws and their relevance to the situations to research and consider, strategies to plan. Instead, she opened her briefcase and removed the sheet of yellowed stationery. Even though she'd memorized every word, she read it again.

This morning, Henry and I returned to the lighthouse . . .

Despite her difficulties, Anna O'Shaughnessy had known what was important. She'd done what she had to do for her child.

Caroline pictured her mother in her mind. Elsa was an old-fashioned name for a woman who'd died far too soon. It was a tragic story, but Caroline's neat and tidy existence seemed tragic, too. She wished there was someone she could talk to. She had so many decisions to make. Her grandfather's house felt empty these days. Despite the magnificent views, her apartment downtown felt claustrophobic. Work wasn't fulfilling, either. Every morning she woke up thinking there had to be more.

She'd conducted an Internet search and had discovered that a town called Harbor Woods was located on the Lake Michigan shore near Charlevoix in northern Michigan. She'd found an address there for a Karl Peterson, too.

Caroline smoothed a lock of her auburn hair between her thumb and forefinger. People often told her she was like her grandfather. He used to tell her she took after her mother. In the journal entry, Anna O'Shaughnessy had implied that Caroline's mother had gotten her red hair from a man named Karl Peterson.

She wondered how her grandfather had felt as he'd read that entry all those years ago. If he were here, she would ask him. While she was at it, she would ask him who she was, because she didn't know anymore.

She knew what she wanted to do, where she wanted to go. She'd known since reading Anna's passage the first time. Her mind racing, her face flushed with possibility, she stood suddenly.

Her plan was bold and spontaneous. She couldn't remember the last time she'd done anything spontaneously. How pathetic was that?

That question gave her the conviction to knock on Edward Hilliard's door. As she entered, her knees shook more than they had when she'd taken the state bar exam. Of course, more was riding on this decision. Her entire future, to be exact.

She sat in the chair Edward indicated. In as few words as possible, she made her request for a leave of absence.

Edward steepled his fingers beneath his fleshy chin. "How long are you planning to be gone? A few weeks?"

"At least," she said. Actually, she wasn't planning to return at all, but she had her child to consider; therefore, she couldn't make rash decisions of this magnitude on a moment's notice. Her grandfather had left her financially sound, but she would have to look closely at her situation before giving formal notice.

"It isn't like you to fly off the handle, Caroline."

No matter what he said, she wasn't flying

off the handle. She was testing her wings. For the first time in her life, she was flying into the wild blue unknown that was her future.

And it had only taken her forty-three years.

CHAPTER 3

A week after requesting a leave of absence from the law firm, Caroline knocked on the door at 408 Prospect Street in Harbor Woods, Michigan.

The house was modest and old. Like the others on this block, it sat close to the street in the shade of large trees. A few of the neighboring homes had issues with peeling paint. Most had small front porches and windows that were open to the breeze blowing off Lake Michigan half a mile away. The windows of this house were closed, the curtains drawn.

As she waited, she glided her fingertips across the letters etched in the mailbox. *K. Peterson.* Had he scratched the letters into the metal or had someone else? She'd found no record that he'd ever married or had children. Wondering about his life, she knocked again.

He didn't appear to be home.

Now what?

She'd spent the night in a bed-and-breakfast inn on Harbor Drive. Until yesterday, her familiarity with Michigan had been limited to her association with fellow attorneys in Detroit, its sprawling suburbs and satellite cities devoted to the automotive industry. The Michigan she'd encountered along the three-hundred-fifty-mile drive from Chicago was something else entirely. She'd passed through harbor towns and woodlands, over sand dunes and past scenic overlooks and signs advertising blueberry festivals and wineries and artist communities.

According to the brochure in her room, Harbor Woods had begun its existence as a fur-trading post at the base of a knoll overlooking Lake Michigan. As the town grew and prospered, it spread up the hill and beyond. The higher the houses sat, the more prominent and prestigious they were. Prospect Street was located near the foot of the hill.

Caroline noticed a woman in a floppy straw hat watering flowers next door. Large-boned, she wore a simple housedress and stockings rolled down below her knees.

"Hello!" Caroline called.

Silence.

Trying again, Caroline said, "Could you tell me where I might find Karl Peterson?"

Again, the woman said nothing.

"I'm Caroline Moore. My grandparents spent a summer here a long time ago. They knew Karl. Does he still live here?"

"What're their names?"

"Henry and Anna O'Shaughnessy."

"Who?"

Easing closer, Caroline removed her sunglasses. "My grandmother died before I was born. Her name was Anna. Henry O'Shaughnessy passed away five weeks ago."

"Never heard of them."

"I'm sure Karl Peterson would remember them. Do you know where he is?"

Squinting until her eyes were mere slits, the woman looked Caroline up and down and up again. "Talk to Shane."

"Shane?" Caroline asked.

"Shane Grady."

"Where might I find him?"

"At the marina, where else?" The woman heaved her large frame around and shuffled up the porch steps and into her house.

Apparently, the conversation had ended.

"It was nice chatting with you, too," Caroline sputtered under her breath as she returned to her car.

Next stop, the Municipal Marina.

"Excuse me. I'm looking for Shane Grady."

Shane had seen the woman walking up the boardwalk, and in one glance had taken in her appearance, from her sunglasses to her Haan loafers. He'd bet his next paycheck she was old money, and old money always spelled trouble. Hair the color of chestnuts skimmed her collarbones. Her shirt was open at the collar and her slacks sat tidily on her hips. She probably considered her attire casual. She was a looker, but city, definitely city. Chicago maybe, or Boston. He would just steer her toward the yacht club, and get back to work.

He shouldn't have been out here on the pier in the first place, but he'd taken a call from his ex-wife, and being outside was one of the few things that made such conversations bearable. Not pleasant. Just bearable.

His cell phone beeped in his hand. Gesturing to the woman that he would just be a moment, he pushed the proper button and said, "Whatcha got, Bobby?" He lifted his field glasses to his eyes. "I see it." Running a finger down the list on his clipboard, he located the name that went with the aging yacht requesting a slip. "He reserved number seventy-three."

An air horn gave two short belches as a big boat chugged past. Shane automatically waved at Dan Bentley and his group of vacationers heading out for an afternoon of charter fishing. A little farther out, two Jet Skis crisscrossed paths parallel with the shore.

The cell phone beeped again. "A guy here just missed that charter, Shane. What should I tell him?"

"It just left Dock three. Tell him the next one leaves at —" he checked his watch "— twelve o'clock."

"I've got another —"

"Hold that thought, Bobby. I'll get back with you."

He could feel the woman watching him. Finally giving her his attention, he said, "Okay. What did you need?"

She removed her sunglasses and pinned him with the bluest eyes he'd ever seen. "Are you Mr. Grady?"

"The only person who calls me mister is my kid's principal. And that's never a pleasant experience."

"Shane, then?" Caroline had asked three people where she could find Shane Grady, and all three had jumped to attention at the mention of his name. She'd expected to find someone businesslike. Someone who wore socks. Someone who didn't give all beards a bad name.

"If you're looking to rent a slip," he said, "you might prefer the accommodations at the Yacht Club. I'd do it soon. They fill up in July and August."

"I'm not interested in accommodations."

His gaze sharpened. "What are you interested in?"

They seemed to be getting off to a bad start. Reeling the conversation back to the issue at hand, she said, "I'm Caroline Moore."

His Nextel beeped again. He held up a finger. "I have to take this one. I'm here, Dave."

He rifled through papers on the clipboard again and rattled off another slip number. "He wants the engine serviced. As soon as they dock, take the boat on over to maintenance. Give it the VIP treatment."

He looked at her again when the call ended, his expression a prod if she'd ever seen one. "Now, what can I do for you —" he glanced at her left hand "— Ms. Moore, is it?"

"Caroline. I'm looking for Karl Peterson."

There was a palpable silence despite the speedboats idling away from the pier. "The lighthouse isn't for sale."

"Lighthouse?"

When his cell phone beeped again, he swore under his breath but didn't answer it. "What's your relation to Karl?"

She wanted to ask him the same thing. Instead, she said, "I'm pretty sure he's my grandfather."

Before the phone could interrupt him again, he turned it off and very quietly said, "I'm listening."

All around her the mid-June hubbub of a busy marina in a tourist town carried on. Another air horn sounded. Seagulls screeched, boats chugged, voices called, and flags whipped in the wind. She wasn't sure what to make of Shane's battered baseball cap and beard, but the way he settled his hands on his hips bespoke of an acquired patience.

"Karl never mentioned a granddaughter."

"It's a long story. Are you two close?" she asked.

"He used to take me fishing."

"Is he a fisherman?" she asked.

"He was a friend."

"Was?" she asked a little too loudly. She hadn't considered that the elderly man might not be alive. "Is he — ?"

"He's alive."

"Thank God." She detected a softening in

41

him, as if he shared the sentiment.

"This isn't the time or the place," he said. "Can you meet me at Chinook Pier later?"

"Chinook Pier?"

"It's a square downtown where residents and tourists can get an outdoor table and listen to the local bands. Eight o'clock?"

"I'll see you then." Caroline retraced her footsteps. For some reason she looked back when she reached the end of the dock. Shane stood at a slight angle facing the water, his field glasses to his eyes, his two-way radio close to his face.

He didn't trust her, that much was obvious. Discovering the truth was going to be more complicated than she'd thought.

Shane Grady was late. Either that, or he wasn't coming.

Caroline had arrived at Chinook Pier a few minutes early. She'd had her choice of tables and had selected one away from the live band, where she and Shane could talk without yelling.

Although it was called Chinook Pier, it wasn't a pier at all, but rather a courtyard with a nautical theme. It was surrounded by gift shops, dress boutiques, specialty stores and restaurants. Ordering a lemonade for herself and another for Shane Grady, Caroline settled back in her chair.

She'd never been a people watcher, and yet she found herself studying the families strolling by. Some adults pushed strollers. Others called to little ones racing ahead. She tried to picture herself doing that.

It was beginning to soak in, to feel real. She was going to have a child, and while that thrilled her, it also scared her to death. She'd never so much as changed a diaper. What about playgroups and nursery school and skinned knees? What about boyfriends or girlfriends and college? How did people do this?

Across the courtyard a family was eating ice-cream cones. A baby slept in some sort of knapsack strapped to the mother's chest while the father showed two other children in an oversize stroller how to lick the ice cream before it ran down their hands. It seemed to Caroline that babies required a great deal of paraphernalia. She wondered if all those apparatuses came with instructions.

"Been waiting long?"

A week ago she would have started. Tonight, she simply turned her attention to the man taking the chair across from her.

Shane had changed his clothes. The ball cap was gone and he wore faded jeans, his deck shoes replaced by comfortable-looking sandals.

She reached for her leather tote hanging on the back of her chair and removed a photo album. Slowly, she slid it toward him. He looked at her for several seconds before opening it.

"My parents died in a plane crash when I was eight years old. I went to live with my grandfather in Chicago." She pointed to the black-and-white photo of three young friends taken on a white beach. "I believe that's him, Henry O'Shaughnessy. And that's my grandmother, Anna. I think the other man is Karl Peterson."

She studied Shane's expression. At his nod, she continued. "Other than wanting to know everything about what my mother and father were like when they were alive, I didn't ask about my family tree. But after my grandfather died last month, I discovered something written by my grandmother."

He scanned the copy she handed him, then began again, slower this time. When he'd finished, he said, "This doesn't prove anything."

"Perhaps, but it does raise a lot of questions. How do you know Karl Peterson?"

Shane watched a drop of condensation

trail down the outside of his glass. Onstage, a local band was massacring Moon River. But that wasn't what had him on edge. Caroline Moore was trouble. He could feel it under his beard the way he could feel an approaching storm.

"Karl took me under his wing from time to time when I needed it. Now, I'm returning the favor."

She stared at him with those Nordic blue eyes of hers, as if she knew there was more to the story. But she only asked, "Is he well?"

"He's eighty-five."

"Meaning he isn't well?"

He was pretty sure her concern was genuine. "Look. Before his stroke, Karl gave me durable power of attorney."

"His stroke?" she asked. "How is he?"

"Depends on the day."

He watched her absorb the implication. "Being a Durable Power of Attorney for someone is a serious responsibility," she said. "A person doesn't give it easily, and certainly not to just anyone. Obviously, he trusts you."

Beneath her scrutiny, Shane had the strangest urge to fidget. He didn't owe her anything, certainly not his life story, so he didn't tell her about all the yelling his parents had done when he was growing up, all the slamming doors and shattering vases and pitchers, the ear-singeing accusations and recriminations. When it got too bad, Shane had escaped to Karl's house. Weather permitting, they went fishing. To this day it's what Shane did when life got out of control.

"How did you and Karl meet?" she asked.

Shane pegged her as an attorney, and probably a damned good one. She sure didn't give up. Finally, he said, "I grew up on Prospect Street."

He saw the dots connect behind her eyes. "You lived next door."

"How did you guess?"

Reaching for her glass of lemonade, she said, "I think I met your mother today."

He made a disparaging sound. "Did my beard tip you off?"

Her smile was wry as she said, "That and your effervescent people skills."

Her wit surprised him. It had been a long time since Shane had been surprised.

"Would you do me a favor?" she asked.

"That depends."

"Karl Peterson trusts you. I'd like to meet him. Would you introduce me to him?"

He studied her longer than was considered polite. She was trouble, all right. But what the hell else was new?

On Saturday morning Caroline met Shane beneath the portico at Woodland Country Manor. Rain pinged against the metal roof before running through gutters and downspouts. The building was large and newer than she'd expected.

Inside, a shrunken old lady called feebly to Shane. "Hello, Shane, dear."

"Hi, Mrs. Wilson," he answered, squeezing her hand on his way by. Other residents called him by name, too, as did most of the staff.

Walking past people using walkers and wheelchairs, Caroline tried to imagine Henry in a place like this. He wouldn't have had the patience for it, and she was thankful he hadn't lingered in his final years.

"How long has Karl been here?" she asked as they turned down another corridor.

"Seven months." Shane knocked on an open door.

Slowly, they went in.

The man who looked up was old but not bedridden. His hair might have been red when he was young, but now was sparse and white. Relying heavily on a cane, he was reed thin and had probably been tall once.

She searched his eyes for something, for some small indication that his mind was intact even though his body was beginning to fail. He looked from her to Shane, unblinking. Shakily, he held out his hand. "Name's Karl Peterson. Pleased to make your acquaintance." He smiled as if proud of his good manners.

Caroline's hopes fell.

"Who're you?" the old man asked her.

Caroline bent down slightly. "I'm —" For the span of one heartbeat, she thought she saw a flicker of recognition in his watery blue eyes. But the moment passed and her disappointment grew.

"Cat got your tongue, girl?"

In that instant he sounded just like Henry had, and Caroline softened toward him. "I'm Caroline. Caroline Moore."

"Not Carolyn, aye?" he said, lowering heavily into an easy chair. "Caroline. Like North Carolina. Did my basic training there during the big war." Resting the cane on one knee, he said, "How do you do, Caroline?"

Before she could reply, he began talking about a fish he'd caught before lunch. "They say red sky at night, sailor's delight. It's not the night that makes for good fishing. You have to wait until morning to know for sure. The stars were still out when we headed for open water this morning."

Caroline glanced out the window at the cloudy sky. Listening, she didn't doubt Karl's sincerity. His fishing expedition had probably happened exactly as he said it had. But it hadn't happened today.

She would have liked to mention her grandmother's name. Karl lived in the past. Would he remember? Or would it upset him? Before long, he began to nod off, and she and Shane left Karl's room.

"Is he always like this?" she asked in the corridor.

"Sometimes he's quiet, lost in his own world. Sometimes he talks a mile a minute about events most people have forgotten. Once in a while, he knows where he is and what day it is. Those days are hard on him."

She didn't speak again until she was outside. "I'd like to visit him again."

Shane's eyebrows drew down in a frown. "You saw his house. Karl doesn't have a lot of money, and before he got sick, he made sure his lighthouse property was very well protected."

Shane didn't know what he'd expected, but it wasn't her slight shift away from him or the way her shoulders went back and her chin came up a degree at a time. He half

49

expected her to give him a piece of her mind. He probably deserved it. He hadn't meant to offend her. He just wanted her to go back to Chicago or wherever the hell else she wanted to go and leave him with his own problems. God knows he had enough already.

She walked out from under the portico straight into the rain. She didn't use her umbrella or the hood of her London Fog jacket. Her sandals splashed through a puddle in the asphalt parking lot, her hair turning darker by the second.

She stopped suddenly and faced him. "You have family, don't you, Mr. Grady?"

The *mister* grated, but the question chafed his conscience. He thought of his son and his mother. He had uncles in Wisconsin and a sister in Baton Rouge and cousins up the wazoo. "Yes, I have family."

"When I buried the man who raised me, I thought I was burying the last of my family. I don't need Karl's money, and I already own a house I don't know what to do with. I just want to know if it's true, if my grandmother really married Henry O'Shaughnessy because she was pregnant with Karl Peterson's child. Anna died before her twenty-fifth birthday, yet in her short life, she was loved by two men. I was close to Henry O'Shaughnessy, and I'm thankful for that. I want to get to know the only other man my grandmother loved. Before it's too late."

"How do you plan to do that?" he asked.

She was getting soaked. Still, she didn't move. "I'm not sure, but I'd like to walk where they walked, and look at the views they saw. Do I need your permission to visit the lighthouse?"

"Would it matter?" he asked.

She smiled, and it was as if she'd known he would understand. It wasn't the first time her smile sneaked up on him. Somehow he doubted it would be the last.

After she'd unlocked her Mercedes and driven away, Shane ran for his ailing Mustang. She was trouble, all right. Unfortunately, trouble always found him.

Caroline ate lunch in her room and tried to take a nap, but between the rain on the roof and the thoughts running through her mind, a decadent nap remained as elusive as easy answers. The fact was, there wasn't much for a tourist to do in the tourist town in the rain. Donning a raincoat and picking up her umbrella, she did what the other tourists were doing today. She went shopping.

Two hours later her packages lay on a bench in a fitting room too small to turn around in. She had no idea where she would wear a silk dress the color of the inside of a conch shell. In a month or two it wouldn't fit her anyway, but she went out to the three-way mirror for a full-length view.

Another woman was already there. Her body tanned and toned, she had professionally streaked blond hair, acrylic nails and a ring on nearly every finger. Scrutinizing her appearance from every angle, she looked at Caroline through the mirror. "Do these capris make my butt look big?"

"Not at all, but don't take my word for it." Caroline gestured to a man holding his wife's purse.

Evidently, the gleam of approval in his eyes was answer enough, because the woman winked at him. A moment later the man's wife relieved him of her purse and led him away, her nose in the air. Caroline and the other woman found themselves sharing a smile.

"What do you think?" Caroline asked.

"Honestly? I think I'm a little obsessed with my looks and I think I failed my kid and my ex, too, but hell, there's only so much blame one person can handle at a time. Does that answer your question?"

Caroline took her turn at the mirror. "I meant what do you think about this dress?"

Their eyes met and they both grinned.

"Too much information," the woman said. "The story of my life. That dress looks fabulous on you. I'm Victoria Young." She held out her hand.

"Caroline Moore."

"My friends call me Tori. Nice to meet you. Unfortunately, even though not much happens in real estate on rainy days, I need to get back to the office."

"You're a Realtor?" Caroline asked.

"As a matter of fact, I am." She handed Caroline an embossed business card. "The main office is in Charlevoix, but I do a lot of my business here."

Examining the card, Caroline said, "Does your brokerage company handle any summer rentals?"

Tori flashed a perfect set of teeth. "I don't know whose lucky day this is, yours or mine. We handle dozens upon dozens of them. Are you interested in looking at summerhouses in Harbor Woods or Charlevoix?"

"Harbor Woods."

"I'll put together some listings. I could show them tomorrow."

Naming a time, Caroline gave her the address of the inn. Both women headed for their respective fitting rooms. Just before closing her door, Tori said, "By the way. Nice shoes."

CHAPTER 4

The first two summerhouses Tori took Caroline to see were located high on a hill inside the city limits. One had a nice view of Harbor Woods, the other glimpses of Lake Michigan. Both were clean and comfortably furnished. But there was something about the third summerhouse she really liked. Once a guesthouse for the larger estate next door, it rested on a postage-stamp-size lot on the channel that connected Oval Lake to Lake Michigan. Roses climbed the weathered picket fences surrounding the property, and an old flagstone walkway meandered from a narrow gravel driveway to the front door.

Unlocking the door, Tori said, "This cottage has been well maintained, but traffic comes to a standstill whenever the bridge is raised to let the big boats in and out of Oval Lake."

Since Caroline planned to walk everywhere, she wasn't worried about traffic. She had no place she *had* to be all summer. She hadn't taken more than a week or two off at one time in fifteen years. The thought of spending the rest of the summer idle was foreign and a little disconcerting. It wasn't as if she planned to do *nothing,* she reminded herself. Now that she'd met Karl, she would continue to visit him. She was going to begin looking for a reputable obstetrician. And she needed to take care of herself, to be as healthy as she could be for her child.

She told herself everything was fine, that she was fine. She'd been telling herself that for a few months now. And yet something was missing. What? The idea of a traditional family? She almost wished that was it, but she feared that whatever was missing was more vital than that. What was missing was joy and excitement. What was missing was *life.* And she wasn't at all certain how or where to find it.

Holding the door for Caroline, Tori said, "I can see why you like this one. It's charming, isn't it? Those ceilings are open-beamed, and the glass in the windows is original. The stone exterior keeps the house cool even in the heat of summer."

"Hmm." The heels of Caroline's Emilio

Pucci's clicked quietly over floors made of hickory planks, wide and worn.

Tori said, "An artist from New York rented it last year. The year before that an out-of-work soap-opera actor stayed here. Movie stars summer up here, you know. Don't expect to see them. At least don't expect to recognize them. Without their makeup, they look worse than you and me."

Tori's left eyebrow rose a fraction, her glance opaque and slightly sheepish. "I didn't mean that quite the way it sounded."

Caroline had come into contact with hundreds of women over the years. Most in her profession were focused and highly competitive. Tori Young was beautiful and bright, yet beneath the acrylics and enhancements was a thread of authentic self-deprecation Caroline couldn't help responding to.

"Do I have lipstick on my teeth or what?"

It wasn't like Caroline to be caught staring. "Of course not," she said. "I was just thinking how rare it is to find such honesty and friendliness. You probably have a dozen friends."

"Don't you?"

It required effort on Caroline's part to let down her guard enough to say, "Recently I took a long, hard look at my life and found it sadly lacking."

"Yeah?" Tori asked. "I take a long, hard look at my life once a day and find it sadly lacking. I'm having a girls' night at my house in Charlevoix tonight. Why don't you come and meet a few of my friends?"

Caroline fumbled for a reply. "I didn't mean to — I'm really not that — what I'm trying to say is —"

"You don't want pity. That's good, because you won't get any from the girls. What you will get is the third degree. If you pass muster, they might even invite you back next week. So, will you join us?"

"The third degree from women I've never met. How could I refuse?"

The gathering at Tori's house in Charlevoix — a town just a few miles away — was a noisy, messy, informal affair. Tori had promised Caroline the third degree, and the third degree was what she'd been getting all evening. Two of the three women had missed their calling and would have made excellent prosecuting attorneys.

Elaine Lawrence, the no-nonsense group organizer, was a tall woman with straight brown hair, too-long bangs and two teen-aged daughters. Nell Downing, who'd been friends with Tori since grade school, was a plump kindergarten teacher with a marvelous sense of humor and a son about the same age as Tori's son. Pattie Barber was the only happily married woman in the group. Her two children were still small. Caroline wasn't sure how she knew Tori, but as far as she could tell, Tori Young was the common denominator among all of them.

The friends had been getting together every week for years, and conversation ran as freely as the wine. Caroline lost track of how many times they'd finished each other's sentences.

"We tried taking turns having these gatherings at each of our houses," Pattie said.

"But we all agreed we enjoyed ourselves most at Tori's place," Elaine said.

"It's one of the few things we've all agreed on," Pattie added.

"Ever," one of the others reiterated.

"Normally, we meet on Thursdays," Elaine added. "Tonight we're celebrating the anniversary of Nell's divorce. No matter what we're celebrating, what's said here, stays here."

Caroline met Elaine's gaze.

Eyeing the bottled water Caroline was sipping, Elaine said, "For future reference, do we need to keep you away from booze?"

"For heaven's sakes, Elaine!" Pattie admonished.

But Caroline shook her head. "It's okay. I'm not an alcoholic. I'm pregnant."

Four pairs of eyes stared at her. Four mouths formed four separate ohs.

Out of the silence, Pattie said, "Congratulations?"

Caroline smiled.

Someone else asked, "Your first?"

"Yes."

And Tori said, "I give you fifteen years and you'll agree that kicking a drinking problem would be easier than what your kid will be putting you through then."

"Amen to that," Elaine declared.

"Hear, hear," Nell said.

Digging a business card from the bottom of her purse, Pattie said, "This is the name of the midwife I used when I had Peter and Molly. She's fantastic." Leaning closer, she whispered, "Ignore them. Parents of teenagers are so depressing."

"What about the father?"

"For heaven's sakes, Elaine!" Nell said.

"How are we going to find out if we don't ask?"

Responding to Pattie's humor and Elaine's frankness and Nell and Tori's lively conversation, Caroline said, "It's all right. I haven't had anyone to confide in in a long time. There is no father."

"Sperm donor?" Elaine quipped.

Wine nearly sprayed out of Tori's mouth.

"I'm just saying that if she went that route, she made a good choice. A sperm donor will never cheat on her," Elaine said.

Caroline didn't know how to reply.

As if she couldn't help herself, Pattie asked, "Immaculate conception?"

"That explanation has only worked once," Elaine said.

"Besides," Caroline pointed out, "what fun would that be?"

All eyes were on her suddenly. One by one, four wineglasses clinked.

"She's in," Elaine declared.

"Ditto," Nell piped.

"I agree," Pattie added.

"I told you so." Tori gave Caroline a wink then finished off her wine, as if that was how friendships were decided.

That was it? Caroline thought. She hadn't expected that it would be so easy. She was accustomed to having to work for everything she accomplished. Learning came easy, but everything else had to be earned. She hadn't even realized how lonely she'd been, or how tired of trying so hard to achieve.

Everything she kept tamped down pressed

upward to the surface. Her first instinct was to bury her emotions. Forcing herself to take a deep breath, she began to talk, instead. At first she spoke tentatively about her childhood and her grandfather, but before long, her insecurities about motherhood were pouring out.

"What am I doing? I've never been around children. I've never so much as held a baby, let alone fed one or changed a diaper."

"That part's not difficult," Elaine said. "You feed one end and diaper the other."

"But when? How much? How often?" Caroline asked.

"The baby will let you know," Pattie assured her.

"Babies are a lot like puppies," Nell added. "Surely you've had pets."

Caroline must have looked bewildered. "I held a rabbit at a petting zoo once."

"Oh, dear."

Her misgivings grew.

"You're bright," Nell insisted.

"You'll get the hang of it when the time comes," Elaine agreed.

Either Tori took pity on her or she realized how vague and unconvincing their advice sounded, because she said, "Caroline has a point."

"I do?"

"There are books on the subject," Elaine said. "Hundreds of them."

"But Caroline's right," Tori insisted. "There's nothing like hands-on experience."

Looking from one woman to the next, Caroline said, "I've faced thieves and divorcing couples who'd like to kill each other, and the most intimidating judges in Chicago. The thought of being solely responsible for this baby terrifies me."

"You could sign up for a parenting class," Elaine said feebly.

"I have a better idea," Nell said, standing suddenly. "A friend of mine teaches a life-skills class at the high school. Each student takes a turn being assigned a computerized doll. This doll is programmed to cry as if it's hungry or wet or needs to be burped or picked up. From what I've heard, the doll simulates a real newborn baby. I bet I could get her to loan me the doll for a day or two. What do you think, Caroline?"

"A computerized doll?" she asked skeptically.

"I think it's a good idea," Elaine said. "It's just a doll. Unlike a puppy, it won't piddle on your carpet."

"Or spit up on you like a baby. Or worse."

"And thirteen years from now she won't throw a hairbrush, giving her sister a black

63

eye," Elaine said.

"Or lie to you about why he was late for curfew," Nell added.

"A doll will never have to be coaxed to leave his room and bribed to go out with friends," Tori said, finishing another glass of wine.

Caroline and Pattie exchanged a long look. With a shake of her head, Pattie said, "Like I said. Parents of teenagers."

Once again, Caroline was tempted to smile.

"Care to give the doll a try?" Nell asked.

Eyeing these four women who'd cared for real newborns and each other, some of Caroline's former bravery and self-confidence returned. "Why not?"

How hard could it be?

A baby was crying.

Whose baby? Was she in a restaurant? Caroline must have been dreaming. The crying continued.

She rolled over and tried to open her eyes. Surfacing enough to get her bearings, she remembered the doll. She wasn't dreaming. If only she were.

She must have been insane to think this would be easy. She must have been insane to agree to try it in the first place.

A high-pitched waaa-waaa-waaaa was coming from the makeshift crib in the corner. Nell had been right. It sounded like a real newborn's cry. Caring for it was much more difficult than Caroline had anticipated.

She swung her feet over the side of her bed and sat up. It was pitch-black outside the windows. Inside, every light was on. It was only two in the morning. The night was never going to end.

She padded to the makeshift crib. Being careful to support the doll's head, she picked it up the way Nell had shown her.

"Waaa," said the doll.

Nell and Tori had dropped the doll off that afternoon. It was Nell who'd demonstrated how the baby worked, pointing out the sensors located on the doll's lips, neck, back, tummy and bottom and explaining how they responded to the sensors on the bottle, and two separate diapers. The doll also responded to rocking motions and sudden movements.

Before leaving, Nell had said, "Wear comfortable clothes and don't panic."

Caroline had managed quite well for the first five hours. When the doll cried, she inserted the key, which looked like a round magnet, into the slot on the doll's abdomen. Once the data was recorded in the main sensor, it was up to Caroline to determine the doll's "needs."

Tori had called earlier, and Caroline assured her it was going well. Just then, the doll had simulated a burp, followed by a gentle coo. "Did you hear that?" she'd asked.

"I heard it."

"This isn't as difficult as I thought it would be."

"It's still early. Call me if you need me," Tori had insisted.

After the first two episodes had gone smoothly, Caroline had been confident she could handle one computerized doll in a simulated real-life setting for one night. But then midnight struck and things had gone downhill fast.

Caroline had kept her head the first time the doll hadn't quieted after she'd placed the bottle to its lips, after she'd changed the diaper, after she'd tried burping it and rocking it, after she'd tried everything and nothing worked. After fifteen minutes of solid crying, she'd almost called Tori. Suddenly and miraculously and for no apparent reason, the doll had quieted. Caroline had been afraid to move, fearing the sensors might pick up even the most insidious change in the atmosphere. Reminding herself it was just a doll, she'd tiptoed to the bathroom and got ready for bed. She'd barely closed her eyes when the crying started all over again.

Since then, she'd lost count of how many times the alarm had sounded. Caroline had done everything, in every order, to try to appease the baby.

"Do you want your two-o'clock feeding?" Feeling silly to be talking to a *doll,* she reached into her pocket for the key. Oh dear. Where was the key?

Wondering if it might have fallen out while she'd slept, she started for the bed, only to stop and retrace her steps to the doll. Deciding to pick it up, she cradled the computerized cry-baby in her arm, then went in search of the key.

The doll cried and cried.

Caroline threw back the sheet and looked beneath her pillow. She discovered an earring and a bookmark, but not the key. It had to be here.

"Waaaa," said the doll.

She tore the bed apart.

"There, there." Caroline checked the nightstand. She looked under the bed and behind the dresser. She searched the bathroom and kitchen counter and the dining-room table where her parenting books were all open. Where on earth was that blasted key?

She'd rocked the doll the last time it had woken up. Or had that been the time before? She searched the rocking chair anyway. From there, she went down on her knees, and with one hand felt beneath the sofa cushions.

"Waaaa."

Gently placing the doll in the little carrier she'd come in, Caroline tore the cushions off the sofa. The key was the circumference of a quarter and was three times as thick. It couldn't have disappeared into thin air.

She spied a tear in the slipcover. Delving in it with two fingers, she finally came up with the key.

She jumped to her feet and quickly plugged the key into the doll. After that, she tried everything else, from feeding to burping to changing to walking the floors.

The doll cried on.

Should she call Tori or Nell or Pattie or Elaine?

To help her with a doll? She couldn't wake them for that. Could she?

Fleetingly, she thought about putting the doll outside. Instead, she placed the tiny, lifelike object to her shoulder and began to walk, swaying gently.

"Waaaa," said the doll.

She'd graduated from college magna cum laude, but she couldn't even take care of a realistic-looking inanimate object made of plastic and stuffing and Velcro. As the minutes ticked slowly by and the crying changed but never truly stopped, Caroline's eyes filled, too.

Maybe she wasn't cut out for motherhood at all.

Tori Young knocked on Caroline's door. The morning birds were singing and a man's voice carried from a boat on the channel, but no sounds came from inside the cottage.

"She must be in there," Nell said, trying the doorbell for the fourth time.

Cupping her hands next to her eyes, Tori peered through the window. "Oh, my." Sofa cushions were on the floor, drawers hung open, chairs were pulled out, and one end of the tablecloth hung to the floor.

The two old friends exchanged a look. "What do you think happened?" Nell asked.

"Nothing good." If there had been signs of a forced entry, Tori would have been afraid the place had been ransacked.

"Do you know her cell-phone number?"

Nell asked.

"No, but if she isn't answering her doorbell, it isn't likely she'd answer her phone."

"Maybe she's in the shower," Nell suggested. "What are you doing?"

Tori lifted the welcome mat and moved a rock. "I thought she might have hidden a key out here. I'm going in." Removing her credit card from her purse, she slid it along the edge of the door. It took a few tries, but the door finally opened. Together, the women slunk furtively inside.

"Caroline?" Familiar with the house's layout, Tori checked the kitchen. Backing out again, she bumped into Nell, jumped and swore.

"Sorry," Nell whispered.

Shoulder to shoulder, they started down the hall. The bathroom door was open, the shower dry and empty. They tried Caroline's bedroom last.

They found her fast asleep on the bare mattress, one arm beneath her head, the other resting protectively over the doll. Being careful not to trip on the parenting books and bedding littering the floor, Tori approached the bed and very gently shook Caroline's shoulder.

"Caroline?"

It took Caroline a few moments to pry

her eyes open.

"Good morning," Nell called.

"It's really morning?"

"I've had some wild Saturday nights, but from the looks of your place, you win the prize," Tori said.

Caroline sprang up and looked all around. "What time is it?"

"Eight-thirty," Nell said. "How long have you been asleep?"

"Almost two hours this time." She reached a hand to the doll. "She cried most of the night."

"She?" Tori asked.

"Dolly."

"Of course." Tori bit back a grin. "Dolly."

Caroline Moore probably had no idea how comical she looked. Pushing her mussed auburn hair out of her face, she adjusted her satin tank. "I'm pretty sure I flunked Life Skills 101."

Gently lifting the doll, Nell inserted a master key and removed some sort of computer board. "I'll know in a minute how you did."

After Nell plugged it into the terminal in her laptop, Caroline's score flashed across the screen, a line-by-line assessment following. Nell turned it off before Caroline had a chance to read it.

"I killed her, didn't I?"

"It's a doll," Nell said. "It wasn't alive in the first place."

"But I flunked."

"Nonsense."

Tori could tell by Caroline's expression that she knew Nell was lying. The poor woman looked ready to cry.

"Do you know what I think, Caroline?" Tori asked. "I think it doesn't matter what the computer chip says. Computers aren't people and that doll, Dolly, isn't a real baby, but it she were, she would be just fine."

Caroline was an educated woman. And she wasn't taking Tori's word for any of this.

"Before you say anything," Tori said, "You should know that we saw you sleeping just now. Your arm was resting over the doll protectively. You named her Dolly, which suggests an emotional involvement."

"Imagine how you'll be with a real baby!" Nell insisted. "Tori's right. You passed. In fact, you're going to be a wonderful mother."

Caroline dropped heavily onto the bed, the motion disrupting the doll's sensor. The crying started.

"Oh dear," Nell said, holding the computer chip. "It isn't supposed to cry without this."

"The doll must be defective," Tori said, raising her voice in order to be heard over the noise. "No wonder it cried all night."

Nell gathered the doll and everything that went with it. "Welcome to motherhood, Caroline."

"We'll call you later."

"You really think I passed?" Caroline asked.

Nell and Tori both nodded.

"With flying colors," Tori insisted. In the car, she said, "Let's get this doll back to the high school. I have to give Caroline credit, if I'd been her and this doll did this all night, I'd have wanted to throw it in the channel."

She blanched, and Nell, bless her heart, placed a hand over hers. "You're too hard on yourself."

Nell Downing was a kind soul, a defender of anyone and anything hurting. Despite the fact that she'd spent most of her life on a diet, she ate out of loneliness, which proved that life wasn't fair. Not that Tori needed proof. She sighed. Although she appreciated Nell's support, it didn't alleviate Tori's guilt. Computerized dolls weren't the only ones with defects. And sometimes it was a parent's fault. Caroline Moore had worried that she'd flunked Life Skills 101, but deep inside Tori feared she was the one failing at motherhood.

CHAPTER 5

Shane rolled over in his narrow bunk. Somewhere, a phone was ringing. Maybe it was Andy's. He burrowed under his pillow. It muffled the sound, but it didn't make the ringing stop. Giving up on sleeping in, he went up on one elbow. In the far bunk, his son rolled over without waking.

It wasn't Andy's phone. Of course it wasn't. His friends had quit calling a long time ago.

The ringing stopped. When it started up again immediately, Shane got up. There was only one person that insistent. Pulling on a pair of tattered sweats, he grabbed his cell phone and went above deck.

"What's up, Vic?"

"You're the only person who still insists upon calling me that." Even exasperated, his ex-wife's voice was a purr in his ear.

"You're the only person who insists upon calling me before eight on Sundays."

The cabin cruiser rocked beneath his feet. As his legs automatically adjusted to the motion, he could practically hear Karl's voice. *We've got our sea legs, aye, Shane? Lucky for us, there isn't anything so bad that a day of fishing can't help.* Too bad Shane couldn't go fishing today.

"You're scratching your chest, aren't you?"

He almost stopped. "What do you want, Vickie?"

Her sigh came as no surprise. "Did Andy stay in last night?"

"What do you think?"

"The entire night?" she asked.

"I took him out for a burger."

"Our kid spent Saturday night having a burger with his father? What I wouldn't give to have to worry he was out raising hell, ya know?"

Yes, Shane knew.

The marina hadn't quieted down until after two in the morning. He could have used another hour or two of shut-eye. When was the last time he'd gotten what he needed? These days he just tried to stay afloat with what he had.

Andy had turned fifteen last month. He lived with Vickie during the week and spent most weekends with Shane. Although Shane kept a house on Elm Street, every summer

Shane moved onto his twenty-foot boat, a boardwalk away from work. He liked sleeping on the water. It beat sleeping in that house by himself.

"Did you suggest he call one of his friends from school?" she asked.

"What good would it have done?"

"You have to keep trying," she sputtered. "He's depressed. And your passiveness isn't helping. He needs us."

Us? "Maybe you should have thought of that before throwing in the towel on our marriage."

"Not that again. It's been four years," she said.

As if he hadn't been keeping track.

"Eleven-and-a-half years is a long time to stay in a loveless marriage, Shane."

Not eleven years. Eleven and a half. She made being married to him sound like Chinese water torture. Shane clenched his jaw harder.

Church bells rang in the distance, welcoming the Catholics to early Mass up on the hill. When Andy was little, they'd all attended services at the First Church of God across town. It had been another of Vickie's self-improvement projects. It wasn't that Shane had anything against the inside of a church. He enjoyed the organ music and he didn't mind passing the collection plate. He'd just always had better luck talking to God out here. He tried to remember the last time God had listened.

Andy hadn't wanted to go to church after Brian's accident. Vickie insisted it was because it brought back too many painful memories of the funeral.

"I've made an appointment with Dr. Avery."

"What are you having done now?" he asked automatically.

"The appointment is for Andy. Dr. Avery is a psychiatrist specializing in teen depression."

Shane nearly bit through his cheek. "You've decided that, have you?"

"I — we have to do something. Do you have a better idea? Because I'm open to suggestions here."

That was just it. He didn't, but he didn't see how a bona fide shrink would be more effective than the grief counselor they'd all seen after Brian drowned. "For starters," Shane said, "You could stop grilling him about cute girls in skimpy bikinis."

"He told you about that?"

Shane swore under his breath. Of course Andy hadn't told him. "I just know you, that's all."

He watched a flock of seagulls fighting over something dead floating in the water. He shuddered, because that was how they'd found Brian.

Andy and Brian had been inseparable from the moment they'd met in kindergarten. Back then, the Kerrigans had lived down the street from the Gradys. Brian had three sisters, and Andy was an only child. The two boys were closer than brothers. There wasn't a photograph of either of them without the other. Until one day when two boys had gone sailing and only one had returned.

Afterward, Shane had felt guilty for dropping to his knees, heartsick yet thankful that he still had his son. Now he wondered which was more difficult, losing a child suddenly or the way he was losing Andy, one silent day at a time.

He could feel the futility and utter helplessness building. He needed to fight the current and the waves and find the perfect spot to drop anchor, to gaze around him and see nothing and no one except miles of open water. Sometimes life made sense in the middle of nowhere, surrounded by sun and sky and sea. In the midst of those elements, he was just a man, no more important than the fish or the gulls, and no less important, either. But he couldn't take his boat out today. Andy was staying with him for the weekend, and the boy refused to leave the marina. He hadn't gone back out on the lake since Brian had drowned.

"I think you should tell him about the appointment, Shane. He might listen to you."

"He's your son, Vic."

"Meaning?" There wasn't another woman alive who could go from semi-pleasant to snide faster than his ex-wife.

"If Andy doesn't want to open up, it won't matter how good the shrink is, any more than it mattered how good the marriage counselor we saw was."

She told him to f-off a split second before she broke the connection. It was the way most of their conversations ended.

Shane was staring into the distance when he noticed the flicker of a shadow on the cabin wall, and he knew that Andy was up. Teenaged boys weren't supposed to be so quiet and light on their feet. They were notoriously messy and noisy and hard on furniture and clothes. Andy was different.

"What'd Mom want?"

Facing the boy, Shane said, "How'd you know it was your mother?"

"The only two people who make you look like you just smelled something rotten are

80

Mom and old man McKenna. And school's out for the summer."

Shane took a good look at his son. For years he and Vickie had been saying that one of these days Andy was going to grow into his feet. He finally had. He'd dressed and combed his hair. As tall as Shane now, he had his mother's nose before her nose job. The rest of his features were practically identical to Shane's at that age. But Shane hadn't been nearly as smart or half as quiet. Andy never raised his voice. He was the most sullen, respectful, hardworking teenager on the planet. Shane didn't remember the last time Andy had smiled and meant it. He kept everything inside, the good and the bad. Maybe Vickie was right. Maybe it *was* eating Andy alive. What if talking about Brian's death made it worse? What then?

"Your mother was wondering how you are. You're up early."

"I've gotta wax the Carmichaels' cabin cruiser today. What did Mom really want?"

Shane didn't know what to say, because deep inside, he knew that Vickie wanted to know that Shane believed Andy would get past Brian's accident. It was what she'd wanted for two years now. She wanted a normal kid, one who acted tough with the guys and flirted with the girls, one who did all the ordinary things kids did. Instead, their son was polite and quiet and did whatever was asked of him. Andy could have won Teenager of the Year Award. Sometimes in the dead of night Shane woke in a cold sweat, because deep down he feared that that wasn't the statistic Andy was going to claim.

Vickie was going to send him to a shrink. And she wanted Shane to tell him. He couldn't bring himself to do that yet.

"She's your mom and she loves you. She wanted to know if you slept okay."

There was a moment of awkwardness between them, as if Andy wanted to say something but didn't know where to begin. The moment passed, and the boy started up the dock.

"Hey, Andy?"

Andy's thin shoulders tensed, his back straightened, as if he was preparing for something unpleasant.

"I bet I could get you out of work today," Shane said. "You know, pull a few strings. Even though I've heard the boss is a real dickweed."

"I've heard that, too."

Shane was the boss, and there wasn't anything he wouldn't have given to see Andy's smile reach his eyes.

"Thanks, but I might as well work today."

It was summer. Andy lived in a resort town where the great outdoors beckoned. And he was winter-pale.

"What about you, Dad? What're you going to do today?"

"I think I'll take the boat over to the lighthouse."

Andy stared at his father for a long time. "You always told me not to dive and swim alone."

His son knew him well.

"You could come along."

For a second, Shane believed Andy might consider it. He didn't realize how badly he wanted that until the moment passed and Andy said, "I've gotta get to work."

"Okay. I'll be careful, son. I promise." And Shane would be. Andy wouldn't survive that kind of tragedy twice.

Shane whisked his shirt over his head. By the time he'd shed his shoes and jeans, he could practically hear the elements calling him.

Fifty yards from shore, a rock formation rose up from the lakebed like an ancient monolith. At night as the sun was setting behind it, it looked like a pensive, hump-backed giant. During the day, it looked exactly like what it was: a misplaced cliff designed by nature, complete with natural steps for climbing. On top, the surface was flat. Twenty feet below was a deep and protected obstacle-free pool perfect for diving.

Leaving his clothes, towel and shoes on the beach, he waded into the lake. Damn, it was cold. He dove under then began swimming, his strokes strong, his mind focused on his surroundings and destination.

As soon as he reached the rocks, he hauled himself out of the water. The boulders were already warm from the sun. He started up as he had at least a hundred times, then stood statue still at the top while the wind and the sun dried his skin and hair.

He'd been a champion swimmer in high school. He'd competed for a while in college, too, but he'd given it up in order to work. He'd given college up eventually, working two jobs in order to support a family.

Eleven and a half years is a long time to stay in a loveless marriage, Shane.

That was just it. It hadn't been loveless on his end.

He walked to the edge. Knees bent, he pressed his toes into the rock's hard surface, pushing off into a perfect arch, hurtling through the cool morning air. This was what he'd needed. To be airborne, to feel this adrenaline rush, to think of nothing but the color of the water rising up to meet him and the sound of the atmosphere rushing past him.

The shock of the cold water stunned him the way it always did. Cutting deeper and deeper, he was just a man, holding his breath, letting gravity and propulsion carry him. And then, in one simple, instinctive motion, he changed course and headed to the surface for air.

Caroline slowed to a crawl, her car creeping over the bumpy country lane. The road beyond the intersection she'd passed a mile back was no longer used. According to the locals, the lighthouse had been abandoned seventy years ago when a taller, more efficient structure had been built a mile up the shore. This was one of the few lighthouses in Michigan to be privately owned. And it belonged to Karl Peterson.

A weathered No Trespassing sign was nailed to the dilapidated gate. Judging from all the tracks in the dusty lane, she wasn't the only one who ignored it. Beyond the gate was the lighthouse from her grandfather's black-and-white photo.

Leaving her car near the door of the connecting cottage, she reached into her pocket for the skeleton key she'd found in her grandfather's desk, and tried it in the lock. The door opened with a loud creak. It took a moment for her eyes to adjust to the dim interior. Dust and cobwebs hung from the rafters and simple furnishings. She tried to picture it the way it had been when her grandparents were young. Had they laughed and played here? Loved here? Although their histories were still sketchy, Caroline had learned that both Karl and Henry had lived in Harbor Woods as children. Anna's family came from Racine, Wisconsin. Every summer, she and her parents had vacationed here.

Some people were drawn to lighthouses. Was the allure the lighthouse itself, or the idea of privacy and seclusion and a time gone by? Obviously, she wasn't the only person who had come here, as evidenced by the writing on the walls. Jason + Jenny. Ben loves Amy. Sue & Chuck 4ever. Caroline had never written her name in such a manner, and lately she wondered what she'd missed.

She wanted to feel young. She wanted to feel everything, and that wanting scared her, but not enough to try to stop it.

She should have been exhausted after her harrowing night with that doll. But the knowledge that she'd passed some unspoken, unwritten test made her feel as if she were on the brink of discovering something wonderful, something exciting, something wild and new.

Sunlight spilled from windows near the ceiling in the lighthouse tower. Weathered oars, old life preservers and rusted lanterns hung on the wall near the circular staircase. She tested the railing, and then she went up. Turning in a circle at the top, she was drawn to a bank of windows and the view of the lake. The water was blue-gray today, the sky a dozen shades lighter. She'd grown up on the same great lake, and yet it looked different back in Chicago. There, sailboats, steamers, tugboats and cargo ships were always moving across the horizon. Here, the horizon was empty of everything except water and sky and a lone rock formation fifty yards from shore.

If she hadn't been looking, she wouldn't have seen the man standing on top of it. She stepped closer to the window. He was wearing dark swim trunks, but it was the way the sun glinted off his dark hair and beard that captured her attention.

The significance of that beard registered

at the same instant he went airborne. And it was as if she was in the air with him. A moment later he sliced into the water. She held her breath, waiting for him to surface.

He came up for air, then splashed around for a few minutes, playing. She thought he might climb up for a second dive. Instead, he swam for shore.

Intrigued, Caroline retraced her footsteps down the spiral stairs. From the cottage doorway, she watched Shane Grady trudge through ankle-deep water, eventually reaching for the towel he'd left in the sand.

She barely knew him, yet after watching him dive, she felt a surprising kinship with him. She wanted to tell him that she understood, not everything certainly, but something. She'd felt as if she'd been on top of that rock with him. And she'd never experienced that before. She was experiencing a lot of things she'd never felt before, and spontaneity was one of them. It felt bold. It felt exciting. And it felt good.

She was about to call out to him, but he reached for the waistband of his swim trunks. Realizing he planned to change into dry clothes before her very eyes, she backed inside, giving him his privacy. With a shake of her head, she told herself excitement was fine, and so was boldness, but spontaneity might not be such a good idea after all.

CHAPTER 6

Shane was towel-drying his hair when he noticed Caroline's Mercedes parked outside the lighthouse cottage. He hadn't planned to stick around, but changing course, he went to look for her. He found her in the lighthouse reading graffiti on the walls.

He stopped in his tracks when he saw her. She could have been a walking advertisement for a high-end boutique in her white shirt and long flowered skirt. She didn't look startled by his presence.

"For the record, you're trespassing."

She made a point of looking at the names etched into the wall, saying, "It appears I'm not the only person who's ever ignored that No Trespassing sign."

Giving her a wide berth, he went to the window and threw it open. "You're probably not the only person to ignore it this week. What are you doing here?"

She looked at him as if wondering how

fortuitous it would be to reply. "That's a good question. Did Karl ever marry?"

He'd bet his next paycheck that wasn't what she'd wanted to say. But he answered, "No, he didn't."

"Pity."

"Is it?" he quipped before he could stop himself.

"How long have you been divorced?"

"Four years. What about you?"

"I never tied the knot, therefore I've never had to untie it." She looked at him. "This is your opportunity to share the wisdom of your experience. Aren't you going to tell me how much trouble and grief I saved myself?"

"No."

"You loved her."

He shrugged. "After we found out she was pregnant, I did the right thing and married her."

"It's hard to believe something built on such a solid foundation didn't last."

Shane almost laughed, and it surprised him. Caroline was looking at him with blue eyes that saw God only knows what. More than he wanted her to see, that was a given.

"You must have been young," she said. "Are you sorry?"

"That I married Vickie and had a child with her? My son is the most important thing in my life. I'd do anything for him. Vickie and I had another argument about him a little while ago."

"I'm afraid I don't have any advice to offer there. I couldn't even take proper care of a doll last night."

"Did you say doll?"

"It was one of those computerized dolls they use in high school Life Skills class."

She acted as if she thought the explanation made sense, so he let the subject drop. Watching her walk in the opposite direction, he wished . . .

What, that she'd turn around and walk toward him, that if he opened his arms she would walk right into them? What then? Forget it. Wishing was futile anyway. He didn't know what was wrong with him. Okay, he knew. He liked the way she looked and he liked the way she held her ground and the way she made him feel. And that was as far as this train of thought was going to go. He had an emotionally wounded son to worry about, a difficult ex-wife, and help that didn't show up for work half the time. His mother had left a message. Heaven only knows what she wanted now, and somewhere in the middle of everything else, he had to make an appointment to meet with Karl's caregivers. Caroline Moore was a complication, plain and simple, and he didn't need any more of those.

"Anna and Karl's names are here," she said. "Anna plus Karl. July the eighth, nineteen forty-two."

So it was true. Karl Peterson had always seemed old to Shane. But he'd been young once, and in love once. It shed a different light on the man. Obviously, it hadn't turned out well for him. When did love ever turn out well for anyone?

"You're not the only one with problems, Shane."

He wondered when his thoughts had become transparent. "I never said I was. What kind of problems do you have?"

She pushed her hair behind her ears then folded her arms as if trying to decide how much to tell him. "For starters, I'm this close to making partner and I'm pretty sure I'm going to throw the opportunity away."

"You call that a problem?"

"And I'm pregnant."

Okay. She had his attention. "You're with someone then?"

"No."

He happened to glance up at the wall, and couldn't look away. A memory washed over him. For a moment, he was young again and everything he wanted was attainable. Land-ing hard back in reality, he said, "My son's staying with me this weekend. I'd better get back to the marina."

"Shane?"

He looked over his shoulder after reaching the door.

"I saw you from the lighthouse tower. I didn't mean to intrude, but I think I understand why you do it. Why you dive."

"Why do I?"

"In one instant you went from air to water. One split second can change everything."

Caroline could practically feel the battle taking place inside Shane. He planted his feet, as if he didn't trust them to stay put otherwise. Although he didn't say it, she knew she was right about him. It really was as if she'd been with him on the top of that cliff. She didn't understand their connection, and from the look on his face, neither did he.

He finally managed to break eye contact, and glanced at something over on the wall. He'd been looking in the same place before. Without another word, he left.

Caroline remained where she was until she heard his boat engine start. With the sound growing fainter, she walked to the exact spot Shane had been standing. Wondering what he'd seen, she skimmed the graffiti.

Perry loves Amy.

John digs Heather. Peace.

Shane + Vickie 4ever.

Fleetingly, she thought of Phillip, and wondered how the reconciliation was going. She hadn't told him about the baby. Did she owe him the truth? She could well imagine how Brenda would feel about that little bombshell.

Her attention returned to the heart with all the cur-licues. Shane + Vickie 4ever. It seemed she'd met another man who still had feelings for his ex-wife. If Caroline was wise, she wouldn't ignore the writing on the wall.

Karl was snoozing in his special easy chair when Caroline arrived at Woodland Country Manor on Monday.

"I always tell visitors to wake them," a nurse said from the doorway. "They can nap anytime, but visitors are gifts."

The nurse shouldered around her and jostled Karl's shoulder. "You've got company, Karl."

He came awake with a start. Blinking a few times, he smiled at Caroline. Her heart practically turned over.

95

"Name's Karl Peterson," he said.

Back to reality, she accepted his handshake. "Caroline Moore."

"It's a pleasure to meet you. Do you work here?" he asked.

"No." She spoke gently. "I'm visiting Harbor Woods for the summer."

"Where're you from?"

"I was born in Boston, but I've spent most of my life in Chicago." Watching him closely, she said, "Have you ever been to Chicago?"

"Le'me see. Chicago. Seems to me I've been there." He squeezed his eyes into slits trying to remember. "Went with my father in thirty-four. No, it was thirty-five. It was during the Depression, and provisions were in short supply. We needed wicks and oil and such to keep the light going. We took the train down. Got back in the nick of time, too." He seemed to come alive as he spoke, as if he were experiencing it again. "Had a miserable November that year. Sometimes the fog rolled in so thick you couldn't see your hand in front of your face. Once my sister and I woke up in the dead of night to the cries of mariners in trouble. Their ship must have hit the rocks. There was an explosion, and then screaming and more cries. Chilling, mournful sounds. A few minutes later everything got real still.

That was worse." Karl was quiet for a moment, remembering. "The inland seas are treacherous places in storms."

Trying to imagine his life, Caroline lowered to the edge of his bed. "You have a sister?"

"A carrottop like me."

"What's her name?"

"Dolores, but we called her Dee Dee. Three years younger than me, she was. Died of whooping cough when she was eleven. My mother blamed it on the lake and the fog and the long, cold winters. It changed her. I guess something like that changes everybody. She wouldn't have anything to do with the lighthouse after that. My father finally took a job in southern Indiana."

"You left the great lake?"

"Soon as I was old enough, I came back." He stopped talking, his mind, it seemed, far away.

"When did you return?"

He started. "What?"

"When did you return to Harbor Woods?"

"When?" he asked. Trying to remember seemed to frustrate him. "I don't know. A long time ago, that's for sure." His blue eyes were faded and watery, and so it seemed were his memories.

He grew quiet after that. The next fifteen

minutes passed slowly. Caroline sat with him. Together they watched the birds on the feeders outside his window, and listened to the people walking past his doorway. They both looked up as the nurse entered with a small tray. Since Karl was tiring, Caroline stood. Laying a hand on the old gentleman's arm, she said, "It was nice seeing you again. I'll come back to visit soon."

As she entered the hallway, she heard Nurse Miller say, "Here you go, Karl. Your liquid potassium and juice chaser. Bottoms up."

Back in his room, Karl drank the concoction obediently. "Who was that woman?" he asked when his grape juice was gone.

"You tell me," Abigail Miller said.

She could see that he was tiring. Sometimes trying to think was an exhausting endeavor. Just before he nodded off, he whispered a name. He'd already closed his eyes, but she was pretty sure he'd said, "Anna."

Caroline was late for girls' night. She'd told Tori to start without her, and from the sound of things, she had.

She'd visited Karl again this morning. Again, he hadn't remembered her from her last visit. Afterward, she'd called Maria.

Caroline was fairly certain she was going to sell the house in Lake Forest. This afternoon, she'd spent two hours on the phone with appraisers, antique dealers, and a representative from an auction house in Chicago.

"Men!" Tori's voice carried through the screen.

"You've got that right!"

Caroline followed the voices to Tori's kitchen, where she acknowledged one wink and another nod before taking a seat at the table next to Nell.

"We came back here for a cup of coffee," Tori said, swirling her wine. "I excused myself to the restroom. I swear I wasn't gone more than two minutes, and when I returned, he was already stripped down to satin boxers with red lips all over them."

"Ugh!" Elaine complained.

"Exactly." Tori was wearing a flirty skirt with a pink top that didn't leave a lot to the imagination. She could have passed for twenty-six.

"What did you do?" Elaine asked.

"I told him dinner wasn't that good and that when I invited him in for coffee, I meant coffee."

"You actually said that?" Nell gasped, smoothing a wrinkle from her loose-fitting summer dress.

"I speak the truth. And do you know what he said?"

"What?"

"He apologized for the meal and said he wanted to make it up to me."

"How original." Elaine rolled her eyes behind her too-long bangs.

"As if his —" Tori cleared her throat "— could make up for poor service, mediocre food and a really annoying laugh."

Nell popped a bite of cookie into her mouth and said, "Nobody has more dating stories than you, Tori."

Tori eyed Caroline. "I'll bet you have a few."

"Very few."

"What happened with your baby's father?" Elaine asked.

This was a sensitive subject, and Caroline wasn't sure how much to tell them. Opting for the basics for now, she said, "He went back to his ex-wife."

"Ouch," Nell said.

"Are you okay?" Tori asked.

Caroline looked at each of her new friends. She'd known them for two weeks, and already she felt a tenderness for them that surprised her.

"Until I came to Harbor Woods and met

the four you, I thought it was normal to have compartmentalized relationships. Everyone loses touch with college friends, right? I'm an only child. My parents have been gone for a long time, but I had my grandfather and my career. I talked to clients and colleagues at the firm every day. We shared business lunches and conference calls, but the only person who knew me well enough to suspect I was pregnant was my grandfather's housekeeper, Maria."

"You weren't close to your neighbors?" Elaine asked.

Caroline shrugged. "I divided my time between my grandfather's house in Lake Forest and my apartment in downtown Chicago. Other than an occasional ride in the elevator, I never saw my city neighbors. When I think about how fast these past ten years have gone, it scares me. I don't want to wake up old one day and realize I haven't laughed, loved or lived."

"I can't guarantee we can help you with your love life," Nell proclaimed, "but if it's laughter and life you're looking for, you've come to the right place. Isn't that right, girls?"

Tori's and Elaine's replies were less enthusiastic, which made Caroline smile. As the others returned to their earlier conversation, Caroline turned to Nell. "Is Pattie coming?"

"Dave had to work late, but she'll be here. She always is. The rest of us couldn't understand why Tori invited Pattie into the group. She's happily married. She likes her job. She has a good relationship with her mother *and* her mother-in-law. At first glance, she doesn't seem like a misfit at all."

Suddenly Nell seemed to be having trouble eating her cookie. Evidently it wasn't easy to chew around the foot she'd stuck in her mouth.

"It's all right," Caroline said. "I think I understand. You're saying Tori collects misfits."

Nell made a face. "I overeat. Elaine acts tough, but Justin's infidelity is killing her. The fact that Pattie is happily married makes her a rarity in this day and age. She's a misfit among the rest of us misfits."

Caroline thought about that. "And what about Tori?"

Nell said, "I've known her all my life. Even when we were in grade school, she always invited every girl in the class to her birthday parties. Some kids thought she wanted presents. But really, she never wanted anybody to feel left out. She wears her heart on her sleeve. Sometimes it causes problems for her."

Just then, Pattie entered the kitchen. Handing her a glass of wine, Tori continued speaking to Elaine. "I'm not saying they don't have their uses. I'm just saying most men place a lot more value on them than they should."

"I'm surprised they don't insure them," Elaine said dourly.

"Who says they don't? Don't get me wrong. They can be a real source of entertainment."

"If you're in the mood for that sort of thing," Nell called from the table. "But day in and day out? You'd think they could give it a rest!"

"Every man I've ever known acts as if he can't function without adjusting it."

"If it isn't in one hand or the other, they're groping for it. Heaven forbid a woman wants to be in control once in a while."

Pattie hadn't even taken her first sip of wine before she said, "Are they talking about what I think they're talking about?"

Caroline nodded.

And Nell said, "The television remote."

Laughter erupted throughout the room. Yes, Caroline thought, joining in. When it came to laughter and life, she'd come to the right place.

"By the way," Tori said above the noise. "Next week we're going to the club."

"Dave has a fit when I go to the club," Pattie complained.

"I can't drink, remember?" Caroline said.

"You're going to be our designated driver." Tori put down her wineglass and began to set out the food.

"What did you do today?" Pattie asked Caroline.

"I went shoe shopping, for one thing. But instead of trying on anything fancy, I bought a good pair of walking shoes. I think I should have picked up new underclothes. All of a sudden, I'm busting out of this bra."

"Enjoy it while it lasts," Tori said.

Caroline was enjoying it. Not the increase in bust size, per se, but all the rest.

"What about you, Elaine?" Nell asked. "What did you do today?"

"I hired a private investigator."

"No kidding?" Nell said.

"I found a receipt for lingerie. Justin hasn't given me lingerie once in the nine years we've been married."

"Oh, Elaine," Pattie said.

"Men," Nell added. "We're better off without them."

"Then why do we keep trying?" Elaine asked.

"That's a good question," Tori replied. "Nell, Elaine, try this crab dip."

Watching her friends across the kitchen, Pattie said, "I'm married to a fantastic guy. He helps with the kids. He compliments me. He's great in bed." She wrinkled up her nose. "But after spending a night with these three when they're in one of their anti-men moods, I don't even like the way he breathes. Have you called the midwife yet?"

"I have an appointment next week. Pattie, did Tori's ex cheat on her, too?"

"I don't think so."

"The other way around?" Caroline asked.

"Tori's not like that. She wanted more is all. More of everything. More than he could give her. I think she feels guilty about that."

"Are you talking about me?" Tori quipped.

"Caroline wants to know if Grady cheated on you."

"He didn't cheat," Tori said.

"As far as you know," Elaine insisted. "He said he wouldn't touch her breasts if she got implants."

Caroline couldn't help glancing at Tori's chest.

"They're mine," Tori said. "For now.

There's always room for improvement, right?"

Sitting in the middle of the aromatic kitchen, women's voices raised in laughter and complaint, Caroline began to understand the dynamics of this group. She rather liked the noise, the disarray, their earthiness. Tori strove for perfection, and yet it was all their imperfections that had brought them together. In Caroline's own way, she'd striven for perfection, too, but it was a mistake, a potentially messy one, that had awakened her to the need to change her life.

And every day, her life *was* changing. She was going to have a baby. She had new friends. She thought of Karl, and fleetingly of Shane. Caroline didn't know what the future held, but she felt breathless and on the brink of discovery. Why, she almost felt young.

CHAPTER 7

Shane could hear boats leaving the marina. A few docks over, a couple of kids were yelling over an idling engine. Below deck it was as quiet as a crypt.

More than a week had passed since Vickie had brought up the subject of the child psychiatrist. Shane had finally broached the subject.

Andy wasn't taking it well. "Dad, no." Even now, he didn't raise his voice.

"Your mother and I discussed this, son. It could help."

Andy darted to the ladder leading to the upper deck. Instead of going up, he stopped there, needing to escape yet needing something else more. But what did he need? If Shane knew that, he might know how to help him.

When Andy was eight years old, he and Brian had found a sparrow with a broken wing. They'd brought it to the marina. "My dad can fix him," Andy had said. "He can fix anything."

That tiny bird couldn't have weighed more than a few ounces, and yet when he'd taken it from his little boy's cupped hands, Shane had felt the weight of a father's responsibility to do the impossible. He felt that weight again.

"What do you mean by doctor?" Andy's voice shook. "What kind of doctor?"

"One who works with kids all the time."

"You mean a child psychiatrist. I'm not crazy."

"That's right, you're not. Ninety-nine percent of the people who talk to psychiatrists aren't crazy."

"I don't want to talk to anybody. I'm doing all right. My report card was better. And Skip says I do a great job on the boats. I'll work harder. You'll see."

"I don't expect you to work harder. You already do the work of three men."

Andy was thin. The baggy jeans and T-shirt made him look forlorn, lost somehow. He didn't smile. How stinking long had it been since his boy had smiled?

"It's Mom's idea, isn't it?"

"We both want —"

"You want what? For your kid to stop being a freak?"

"You're not a freak. You're sad."

Andy looked as if he'd been slapped.

"Sadness isn't an affliction, son. It's a natural process. A necessary process."

"I won't go. She can't make me. I won't. The other day she told me she wants me to whistle again. I'll whistle all day long if it'll get her off my case. Please, Dad. Talk to her. I don't want to go to a shrink. I won't."

That was three won'ts. Shane felt wrung out. This was the most he'd gotten out of his son in a long, long time, but instead of making Shane feel better, he only felt more unsure.

"Mom would be happier if she found a joint in my pocket and smelled beer on my breath. I could do that, but I don't. Does she appreciate it? Instead, she doesn't like having a freak for a son."

His mention of pot startled Shane. And Andy was really hung up on this freak thing. "That's not true and you know it," Shane said. "She wants you to be happy again, the way you were before." It was the closest they came to mentioning Brian's accident. "It's what I want, too."

Andy took a moment to regain his composure. "You'll talk to her?"

Shane could practically feel that little bird's heart beating against his hand. "We both love you. You know that, don't you?"

"Then call her off."

Shane hated this. This uncertainty. This being put in the middle, between Andy and his mother.

"Please, Dad?"

"I'll talk to her."

Andy didn't gloat. Shane doubted it was in him anymore.

"It doesn't mean we won't address this again in the future."

The boy looked relieved as he said, "I've gotta get back to work." Without a sound, he went up on deck.

Shane didn't know if he was doing the right thing. He never knew anymore. He wanted to believe that at least some of Andy's behavior was normal. The kid was fifteen! Shane remembered what that had been like. Sometimes it had felt like being in a dark tunnel. The carefree days of childhood were far behind, and the promise of freedom, of adulthood was far ahead.

Time healed. How many times had they all heard that? Was Vickie right? Could a psychiatrist help Andy more than time could? God. Vickie. She'd have Shane's balls on a platter for this one. It was getting harder and harder to care.

His stomach rumbled, deep and empty.

He eyed the slices of bread he'd gotten out before he and Andy had started talking. He'd planned to make a peanut butter sandwich and get back to work.

He had to get out of there, go somewhere, be somewhere, anywhere but here. Sweeping the bread off the galley counter and into the trash, he hurried to the upper deck for some fresh air.

Shane took his foot from the accelerator, coasting. Caroline Moore was walking up ahead. He'd known it was her from a block away. She was a class act from the tip of her auburn head to the heels of whatever expensive shoes she was wearing today. She was heading south, toward the Oval Lake Bridge. Lunch was north.

He'd planned to go straight to Clara's Diner, where he would polish off a plate of pan-fried whitefish and warm peach cobbler. He would sit alone. He would eat alone. He wouldn't talk. And he wouldn't think.

He stopped at the curb. "Need a ride?"

The wind blew a section of her hair across her cheek. Even from this distance, he could see the indecision in her eyes.

"You can bring your mace."

She lost the battle of personal restraint,

111

and smiled. "In that case, how could I refuse?"

Once she was settled in her seat, he checked his mirrors and pulled into traffic. "Where to?"

"I'm renting a summerhouse on the channel."

He could feel her looking at him as he eased into the center lane. She probably sensed his agitation. Instead of commenting, she looked out the window.

They rode in silence until Shane spied the flashing lights up ahead. "They're raising the bridge. I hope you're not in a hurry to get there."

"I'm not in a hurry." Her sigh filled the car.

Sweat trickled down the side of his face. Old Shelby Mustangs didn't come equipped with air-conditioning. The radio didn't work, either. Normally, it suited Shane just fine. For some reason, he felt the need to fill the silence today.

"Andy and I just had a talk. His mother wants him to start seeing a psychiatrist. I'm supposed to make him go."

"And you don't want him to go?"

"I don't know what's best. He doesn't want to go." Shane found himself telling her about Brian. "Knobby knees and freckles,

Brian had a cowlick right here." He pointed to a spot on his own forehead. "He was always skinning his elbows or his shins. Laugh. You should have heard those two boys laugh. Andy doesn't laugh anymore."

"What happened?" she asked.

"Brian drowned."

From the corner of his eye, he saw her hand cover her mouth.

"It happened two years ago. It was a windy day, perfect for sailing. They took the Kerrigans' catboat out. Brian's father watched them go. He said Brian was wearing his life jacket. They both were. We don't know why Brian took his off."

Shane was reminded of something Caroline had said yesterday, about why he dove. *One split second can change everything.*

"A sudden gust of wind came up, catching the sail. It pitched Brian out of the boat. It must have knocked him unconscious. Andy saw him go under. Brian didn't come back up for two days."

Shane concentrated on the perspiration running down the side of his neck and not on the image trying to burn itself into his mind. "Both boys were avid sailors and strong swimmers. Andy went in to try to save Brian. He wishes it had been the other way around, that he'd been the one to die that day. His mother's worried about him. Hell, who isn't? She wants him to see a psychiatrist and I just caved and told him I'd talk to her."

The breeze stirred Shane's short beard. Up ahead, the bridge was being lowered. He watched the tall sailboats that had just been let into Lake Michigan. "We used to spend hours together, Andy and Brian and I. We had fishing gear, sailboats, Jet Skis, and all the toys families with kids need to spend all their free time on the water. Andy thinks I sold everything, but I put most of it in storage, hoping he'd want it again someday. I don't know if I did the right thing. That's the trouble with parenthood. You never know."

Caroline didn't agree or disagree. Other than making an occasional sound to let him know she was listening, she didn't say much of anything. Perhaps that was why he kept talking. And talking. By the time he stopped, he was sitting on a stool in her kitchen, and an hour had passed. *An hour.* He had to look at his watch twice to believe it. It wasn't like him to take an hour for lunch. He knew he should be getting back to the marina, but he didn't get up.

"Help yourself to another cookie," she said, after he'd already taken a bite of another one.

He hadn't expected to smile. Not today. "I've done all the talking."

"Is that unusual for you?"

Finally standing up, he said, "Very."

"Maybe taking your son to see a psychiatrist isn't a bad idea. You said he won't go in the water."

"That's right."

"And yet he works at the marina and sleeps on your boat when he stays with you? How does he get there?"

"He rides his bike."

"All the way from Charlevoix?"

He nodded, wondering where she was going with this.

"He must like to ride."

Shane's mind raced. Years ago he'd had a sixteen-speed trail bike. He tried to remember what had happened to it. "Every year on Labor Day thousands of bicyclists ride across the Mackinaw Bridge. There are probably bicycling clubs, marathons, plotted courses. Maybe Andy and I could ride together. I keep thinking if only he could reconnect with somebody. Maybe this would be a start."

"Maybe."

"It's possible you're a genius."

She sighed.

"Something on your mind?" he asked.

"I saw the midwife for the first time this morning."

"Did everything check out?"

She carried their snack plates to the sink. She'd kicked her sandals off near the door when they'd arrived. One sat upright, the other was tipped on its side. Without them, the bottoms of her light blue pants brushed the floor. A little farther up, the fabric hugged her curves and followed her every move.

"I walked into that office feeling young. I walked out practically needing a cane."

"Was the midwife fresh out of college or something?"

"No, she's very knowledgeable and seasoned, exactly what I'm looking for. She said I'm approximately sixteen weeks along. Although I'm slightly anemic, my blood pressure is good, and whatever I've been feeling probably isn't the baby."

"I don't see a problem," Shane said.

"Apparently I was her first patient today whose navel isn't pierced."

Somehow Shane doubted she would appreciate it if he laughed. "The other expectant mothers were on the young side, were they?"

"Two of them were still in high school.

There *was* one woman about my age. She asked me how I was handling menopause." She looked at him from across the room. "You'd better not be smiling beneath that beard."

This was one of those impossible situations men often stumbled into. It seemed to him she'd told him she was forty-three. She looked damned good no matter how old she was. If she was four months along, she hid it well.

He couldn't help it that he had to walk past her in order to reach the door. Stopping close to her on his way by, he let his hands settle on his hips. "Know what I think, Caroline?" Giving her a quick but thorough once-over, he said, "I think belly-button rings are overrated."

He leaned in, brushing his lips against hers. It didn't last long enough for either of them to close their eyes. He hadn't planned to kiss her, and he didn't stay long enough to read her reaction. As he drove away, he wasn't sure she felt any younger.

But he sure did.

Four hours later, Caroline caught herself running the tip of her tongue over her lower lip. How many times did that make?

She was on her way to Elaine's house in

Charlevoix, and she, Pattie and Tori were outlining their strategy via their cell phones. Evidently Elaine had proof that her husband was cheating. She'd called Tori, and Tori called the others. They all pulled through the open gate and into Elaine's driveway, parking in single file.

Elaine threw her front door open before Pattie could ring the bell. Caroline, Pattie and Tori entered a grand, two-storied foyer. "We came as soon as Tori called," Pattie said, still in her scrubs.

"Where's Nell?" Elaine's hair was disheveled, her face pale.

"She and her sister took the kids to visit her mother this week, remember?" Pattie said.

"Let's see this proof," Tori insisted.

Although she had yet to change out of her bathrobe, Elaine's hands were surprisingly steady as she handed over a large manila envelope. Opening it, Tori said, "It didn't take your private investigator long to come up with these."

Caroline peered at the black-and-white photographs in Tori's hand. There were five in all. Each contained a date and time, and each one depicted a middle-aged man with a slight paunch and a much-younger woman. One had captured them entering a hotel. The final photograph showed them leaving it an hour and a half later.

"Now you know," Tori said, slipping the photos back into the envelope and out of Elaine's sight. "Now you can divorce his sorry ass."

When Elaine made no reply, Pattie steered her toward a wing chair. "Where are Trish and Tracie?" she asked gently.

"They're at their father's this week. They love their father, but they adore Justin. He's good to them."

"If he wanted to be really good to them," Pattie said, "he would be faithful to their mother."

"You're right. I know you're right." Elaine sighed heavily. "Her name is Brittany. She's twenty-seven."

"It figures." Sinking to the edge of the sofa, Tori adjusted her lime-green skirt around her thighs. "You're much prettier. Which just proves what you already knew. Justin is slime."

"She may not have a pretty face," Elaine said, "but look at her body. He's always been a breast man."

"Oh, honey," Pattie insisted, "you don't deserve this."

"He's slime," Tori insisted.

Caroline was too new to this group to

have formed an educated opinion about Elaine's husband, but she knew firsthand how it felt to discover that the man she'd been seeing was cheating on her. Her heart went out to Elaine.

"Those photographs aren't the worst of it." Elaine's voice sounded hollow.

"What could be worse?" Pattie asked, then rubbed her arm where Tori had jabbed it with her elbow.

"The day those photographs were taken, he kissed me goodbye. I remember that morning clearly. He knew he would be screwing her, but he still kissed me as if he didn't want to leave. It was a long, dreamy, lingering kiss, because the night before, we'd made love."

"You had sex even though you suspected he was cheating on you?" Tori asked as gently as possible.

"I hoped I was wrong."

Wishing there was something she could do, Caroline said, "Why don't I brew some tea? Do you have chamomile?"

Elaine rose shakily. "I think I'll go to bed."

"We just got here," Tori said.

"It's only four in the afternoon," Pattie insisted.

"I appreciate you three coming, but I want to be alone right now. I need to cry, and I don't cry well in front of people."

"We're not people," Pattie insisted. "We're your best friends."

In the end, Elaine wouldn't be swayed. After promising to call her later, Tori, Pattie and Caroline let themselves out.

"Do you think she'll leave him this time?" Pattie asked, on her way to her car.

This time? Caroline thought.

"Who knows," Tori said. "She hired a private investigator. She never did that before. Maybe she'll finally do something about his cheating ways."

Pattie said, "I can't believe Justin kissed her when he had every intention of meeting his mistress a few hours later. That's low. I always thought a man's kiss meant something."

"Life would be so much easier if all women were lesbians," Tori said.

"Whoa. What did your ex do now?" Pattie asked.

"The usual. He comes out smelling like a rose, and Andy treats me like Attila the Hun."

Another Andy, Caroline thought, recalling the name of Shane's son.

"If I were Elaine, I'd find Justin's stash of condoms and inject them with pepper spray. Assuming he uses them."

Pattie glanced at Caroline. "I'm not a man hater, but certain offenses call for just punishments."

"Castration comes to mind," Tori said.

Not a good day for men or exes, Caroline thought. Once again, she thought these women would have made excellent prosecuting attorneys. Obviously they weren't the type to forgive and forget.

"I have to pick up the kids at day care," Pattie said. "I'll call you both later."

As Pattie drove away, Tori turned to Caroline. "I have an hour before I have to show a house. Care to grab a cup of coffee?"

She followed Tori to a little coffee shop on Mason Street. Hurrying to the shade of a sky-blue awning, Caroline looked in both directions. This was her first venture into Charlevoix beyond Tori's house where they met on Thursdays for girls' night. The sidewalks were crowded, and the storefronts in view held a certain charm. "I've been toying with the idea of opening a law practice in Michigan."

"In Charlevoix?" Tori asked, holding the door for her.

While they waited in line to place their orders, Tori told Caroline about the town. It had more than twenty thousand year-round residents — twice as many as Harbor

Woods. Tori had been born and raised here. According to her, before the upscale shops, restaurants and yachts lined the valley, the business district had been referred to as the Mason-Dixon line because most of the land on the north side of the road had belonged to a farmer named John Dixon, and the south side to one named Seth Mason. The land had long since been subdivided, but Dixon Avenue and Mason Street still marked the north and south ends of the downtown district.

"The city's old, but it's changing with the times. We could use a few more good attorneys," Tori said, being careful not to slosh latte over the rim of her foam cup.

Caroline placed her decaf on the narrow table and slid onto the bench opposite Tori. "It would be a completely different world than I'm used to. You wouldn't believe how many times I've wished I could talk it over with my grandfather."

"Was he your mentor?" Tori asked.

"Yes. I always knew his advice was going to be good if he took off his glasses and cleaned them first. This afternoon, I dialed his number without thinking."

"He was your only family for a long time."

Caroline nodded. "And now I have no one, except my baby."

"And don't forget your friends." Tori took out her compact and checked her makeup. "Are you serious about starting a law practice here? Because I don't care if Elaine did sign a prenup, and everything is in Justin's name. She helped him build that business, and she deserves her fair share, and there are probably a lot of other women just like her who could use good counsel."

"I *have* found loopholes in prenuptial agreements before," Caroline said. "But Elaine has to want to leave him. Any idea why she stays?"

"She thinks she deserves his infidelity."

Caroline sat back. "Ah. She knows how it feels to be the other woman."

"I remember when Elaine started seeing him. It was Justin this and Justin that. He told her his wife didn't understand him, that they'd grown apart, that they never should have gotten married in the first place. He said she didn't give him the time of day. He probably tells his lays the same thing about Elaine."

"So you think it's guilt that keeps her in the marriage?"

Tori ran the tip of one fingernail around the rim of her cup. "Guilt is a powerful emotion." Meeting Caroline's eyes, she said, "It haunts you. You probably don't know what that's like."

Keeping her voice very quiet, Caroline said, "My child's father doesn't know I'm pregnant."

Taking a moment to digest that, Tori said, "Are you going to tell him?"

"I tried to tell him after my grandfather died, but all Steven could talk about was how happy his two sons were because he and their mother were reconciling. He was already seeing her by then, and sleeping with both of us. I think it's too late to tell him. Am I cheating my baby? Or is it better this way?"

Tori sighed heavily. "Welcome to the club. I mean that. Where would women be without each other?" Glancing at her watch, she said, "I still have forty-five minutes before I'm meeting my clients. My office is right around the corner. I'd be happy to do an Internet search to see what office space is available."

"You'd do that?"

"I work on commission." Tori winked. "But I give friends a discount."

With a shake of her head, Caroline said, "Lead the way."

Five minutes later Tori was pressing buttons on the computer in her office and Caroline was sitting in a comfortable armchair on the other side of the desk. Tori's office was sleek and tailored. A ficus tree was thriving in front of the room's only window.

Leaving Tori to her Internet search, Caroline went to the bookcase where she saw three framed photos. One was a picture of Tori accepting an award. The other two were of a boy, one when he was five or six, the other more recent. "Is this your son?"

Tori looked over her shoulder. "That's my Andy."

"Do people say he looks like you?"

"He has my old nose."

The boy's nose didn't look bad to Caroline. She wondered what drove women to change their appearances so drastically. She especially wondered what drove Tori.

"He's an only child?"

"His dad and I had to get married. I knew early on that it wasn't going to last and I didn't see any reason to bring another child into it."

"You never remarried?"

"I'm still looking for the perfect man. I've kissed a few toads, believe me."

Caroline thought about that, and about something Pattie had said earlier. "Do you think a kiss always means something?"

"Are you thinking about kissing some-body?"

Returning to the chair and her coffee, she said, "Someone kissed me the other day."

"Are you seeing someone?"

"No."

The computer made a series of clicking sounds. "Don't do this to me," Tori told it. Glancing at Caroline again, she said, "Some guy off the street just up and kissed you?"

"Of course not. It turns out there's another branch on my family tree." Caroline rested her elbows on the arms of the chair, her coffee cup held loosely in both hands. "Recently I learned that I have a grandfather I never knew about. The two men know each other."

"So this guy who kissed you is old?"

Leave it to Tori to ask that.

"He's, I don't know, fortyish."

"So how was it?"

Touching the tip of her tongue to her lower lip, Caroline was sorry she'd brought this up. "It wasn't really even a kiss."

"What was it then?"

"It was barely more than a brush of his beard against my chin."

"What is it with guys and beards? Does this guy who kissed you know you're pregnant?"

"Yes."

"No offense, but that's usually a pretty solid reason for a man *not* to kiss a woman he's just met. So, do you like him?"

Caroline wasn't certain how she felt about Shane. "He isn't like the men I knew in Chicago. I doubt his closet contains more than one suit, and I'm not sure he even owns a pair of socks. But then, Steven had a closet full of both, and look how that turned out."

"You're saying you *do* like him?" Tori had a knack for getting to the heart of a situation.

"It's not as if he's trying to get me into bed. It was just a kiss."

"Trust me, it's never just a kiss."

"As you said, I'm pregnant." Caroline adjusted the lid on her cup.

"I was three-and-a-half months along on my honeymoon, and let me tell you, we couldn't keep our hands off each other."

"You must have loved him in the beginning," Caroline said, taking a sip of her decaf.

"I wanted to love him. I wanted to be in love, you know? I was twenty-two. Shane was twenty-four."

The coffee almost made it down Caroline's throat before her throat closed up.

She coughed, choked, sputtered and coughed some more.

"Are you okay?" Tori asked, hovering over her.

Eventually, Caroline could breathe. It took even longer before she could think. She distinctly remembered Nell referring to Tori's ex as Grady. She'd assumed that was his first name. And the names drawn on the wall in the lighthouse were Shane and Vickie.

Shane Grady.

And Vickie. Victoria. Tori. One and the same.

She knew a total of six people in upper Michigan, and two of them had been married to each other. That was some coincidence.

"He has you thinking about him," Tori said. "Chances are that was his intention."

Bit by bit Caroline's mind was clearing, but she put her coffee down just to be safe. She didn't think that kiss had been planned. Besides, it barely constituted a kiss.

She thought about Shane's situation and the problems he was facing with his son. Andy was Tori's son, too.

Caroline didn't know how a man would feel about seeing a friend of his ex-wife's, but it would matter to a woman. Her fledgling friendships were important. The situation with Elaine drove home just how important. Bad things happened to everyone, but if women were lucky, they had each other to turn to when things fell apart.

Tori's intercom buzzed. "Your clients are here," the receptionist said.

"I'll be right out." Tori straightened her skirt and fluffed her hair. Rising to her feet, she said, "There aren't any vacant office spaces on the main street in Charlevoix, but there are three on adjacent side streets. I'll do a more thorough search and call you tomorrow. Do you think you'll be seeing him again?"

"Not the way you're thinking."

"Uh-huh."

"I mean it." They fell into step in the hall. "Besides, it would only be a problem if I allowed it to be."

"Oh, honey," Tori said just before she turned the corner and entered the lobby where her clients were waiting. "Those are famous last words. Just ask Elaine."

CHAPTER 8

Shane's car was parked in her driveway when Caroline returned from Charlevoix. She saw him near the water, leaning on the iron railing that ran the entire length of the channel. His back to her, he was talking to two men in a covered wooden boat that looked as if it had been wind-tossed in stormy seas for decades.

She'd seen the old boat several times, usually about midday. Its approach was always heralded by the squawking and screeching of seagulls. Tonight it was heading away from Oval Lake instead of toward it. The man at the helm must have alerted Shane to Caroline's presence, because Shane glanced over his shoulder at her. The boat chugged away, and Shane ambled up the sloping lawn, stopping near her.

She was coming to recognize that stance, his hands resting casually on his hips, shoulders squared, head tilted slightly, and yet if he'd been in a police lineup, and she'd had to point to the one she thought was Tori's ex-husband, Shane would have been her last choice. Regardless, they'd been married, to each other. Okay, they were divorced. Steven had been divorced, too. Caroline remembered how Shane had stared at two young lovers' names on the lighthouse wall.

Forewarned was forearmed.

"That was James Pride," he said. "The Pride Fishery is a landmark in Harbor Woods."

Something was different about him tonight. His hair was still brown. His jeans were still threadbare. And he still wasn't wearing any socks. She wished it wasn't so good to see him.

"Is something wrong?" he asked.

"Everything fine, thanks." One awkward moment followed another before she said, "Did you need something?"

"Need's a funny thing."

Caroline felt a gentling in the pit of her stomach. She really *needed* to put some distance between them, figuratively and literally. How could she have gone her entire life without developing such fundamental skills?

"I have some things I need to do. So, um."

Oh for the love of — she sucked at this.

He wasn't especially good at certain things, either, such as taking hints, because he didn't budge. "You were right about me, about the reason I dive. I'd never examined it, but you nailed it. And then, today, you listened."

He wasn't making it easy for her to erect barriers and set boundaries. "You're welcome, Shane. Now, if you'll excuse me."

"Caroline, what's going on?"

He followed her inside and removed the ball cap. He was more refined than she'd wanted to believe. He could be charming when he wanted to be. It sent up another red flag.

She'd told herself she wanted to feel young. She should have been more specific, because this felt like junior high.

"I'm taking your advice," he said. "I found my old bike. Andy and I are going riding tonight."

"He agreed to go?" she asked before she could stop herself.

"He wasn't excited about it, but he agreed to go, yes."

Had he moved closer? Or had she?

She held up one hand, only to lower it again. "Don't."

"Don't," he repeated.

"That's right. Don't try to charm me."

"You think I'm charming?"

She finally realized what was different about him. He'd trimmed his beard. It transformed his features from harsh to handsome. Another red flag went up.

"Don't look at me like that, either, as if you're trying to figure me out, as if you want to *understand* me. I'm not your type, Shane. So just don't, all right?"

It didn't take him long to react, and yet there was simple dignity in the way he took a sheet of paper from his back pocket and placed it on her table. "Have it your way, Caroline."

He left without saying another word, and closed the door just short of a slam.

Caroline didn't move until she heard him start his car and drive away. She was known throughout Chicago for keeping a level head. She didn't overreact in court or out of it. And yet she'd handled things badly today. She was terrible at relationships, but the truth was, she preferred not to get involved with Tori's ex-husband. Wondering what else she should have said or done, she strode to the table and picked up the yellowed paper Shane had left there.

It was a letter addressed to Sergeant Karl Peterson, c/o U.S. Army General Post. The outside was stamped in several places, the last of which was in French. It was from Anna.

After all this time, Caroline held in her hand a piece of her history, and something both Anna and Karl had touched. Carefully unfolding the old stationery, she sat in the straight-backed chair at the table and began to read.

December 30, 1943

Dear Karl,
 So many times I've tried to write this letter, only to stop, unable to bring myself to put the difficult words on paper. I wish there was a gentle way to tell you what I'm about to tell you, but there is none. It's not fair. None of it's fair. Not this war. Not what I must do. Nor is it fair for me to be thinking of you, not now, not anymore.
 Henry and I were married on December 11. He wanted to tell you, but it's my place to do so. He loves me. I don't know why, but he does. I don't know what I would have done without him these past months. I'm trying to do what's best, and still, I don't know how to stop loving you. I must try, for it's

not fair to him or to you.

I haven't heard from you since you came home on leave. For three months I tried frantically to reach you. The army won't tell me where you are. I pray you're safe. I know I shouldn't pray that one day you'll forgive Henry and me, and yet I do. I pray for that most of all. I'm so sorry, Karl. Such inadequate words for the sorrow in my heart. I grieve for the love you and I shared, and I can't help imagining how you will feel when you read this letter. Please believe me when I say I had no other choice. Now I must look forward, not back, and so must you. I beg you, be safe. And please be happy one day.

Anna

Caroline must have read the letter twenty times. In fact, she spent the next two hours doing nothing but reading it, thinking about it, and studying the photograph she'd discovered in her grandfather's attic two months ago. She could imagine each of them as they'd been then: One girl loved by two men, a war, a different era, an impossible situation, and three lives changed forever. In reality, it wasn't only three lives that had been changed. Caroline's life had been affected, too. And now, it would affect her child.

Life was never simple. She used to believe it was, but she'd been wrong. It felt as if her life had been divided into three parts. There was the whimsical first eight years when her parents had been alive, her focused and goal-oriented existence in Chicago, and this new, uncertain, learn-as-she-was-going entity she was experiencing now.

Putting the letter and photograph aside, she asked herself what was important. The answer was crystal clear. Her baby. She'd known it since that wand had turned blue. The emotion, the sentiment, the sheer power of her love was something she'd never felt before. The fact that she'd failed the Life Skills night from hell was immaterial. She was going to do everything in her power to be a good mother.

Voices carried from the channel. Following those sounds to the open window, she saw a large boat floating by on the channel. In the back, a man and woman sat on either side of three little girls. One of the children pointed at something. Whatever she said must have been funny, because they all laughed. As the boat lumbered out of sight, Caroline thought about families.

She was an excellent lawyer. She would learn to be a good mother. But her relationship skills left a lot to be desired. She needed to keep trying, because the riches in life weren't measured by cases won. It seemed to her that the richest lives were those with deep, lasting friendships and family history passed on from generation to generation.

Shane had given her a gift in the form of Anna's letter. And what had she done? Insulted him and practically slammed the door in his face. She owed him something.

Before she talked herself out of it, she reached for her keys.

Shane's was one of the few boats in its slip this evening. He sat on deck, his head bowed as he worked on something in a large plastic case on his lap. The setting sun was a ball of orange beyond him, tingeing the sky pink and lavender, fading to gray.

The cork soles of Caroline's sandals muffled her approach on the wooden pier, and yet something must have alerted him to her presence. He looked up and didn't look away.

"Where did you get the letter?" she asked, stopping where his boat was fastened to the pier.

"Beneath a loose floorboard in the light-house cottage."

"When?"

"Twenty-five minutes before your little *don't* speech."

Despite the fact that she deserved that, she cringed. "I owe you an apology."

"You don't owe me anything."

He wasn't going to make this easy for her. Ironically, it put her on more even footing. "You trimmed your beard, showed up unannounced, and I jumped to conclusions," she said.

There was something deliberate about the way he closed the tackle box and placed it at his feet, something just as deliberate in the way he smoothed a hand over his short beard. "What conclusions?"

He seemed to take perverse satisfaction in making her say it. Fine. "You surprised me when you kissed me."

"I'm listening."

"Why did you?" she asked.

"You insinuated you felt old."

"Then it was a pity kiss?" How lovely.

Waves pressed against the cement pilings of the pier, splashing on the boat's hull, only to be dragged slowly, rhythmically away again. All around them boats were starting to come in.

"What difference does it make?" he asked. "I'm not your type, remember?"

"I didn't say you're not my type. I said I'm not yours. There's a big difference. I'm not good at relationships. In fact, I can count my friends on one hand. I'm figuring this out as I go, but this is my flaw, not yours."

"What kind of flaw?"

"It would take all night to explain."

She caught him looking at her mouth. "Would you care to come aboard, Caroline?"

She shook her head, thinking she should have expected that. Covering a yawn, she said, "All I seem to want to do lately is sleep."

"I was only suggesting you come aboard to talk. Andy's below deck."

Ah, yes, Andy. Shane's and Tori's troubled son.

"Normally he stays at his mother's during the week, but I think he took pity on me after riding my butt into the ground tonight. It's hell getting old. For the record, that wasn't a pity kiss. I talked. You listened. You talked. I kissed you. That's just the way it happened to work out."

And men claimed women were illogical.

Shane wasn't like the men she'd known in

Chicago. There was a vein of the uncivilized in him. Something about him brought out the worst in her, and the best.

She wasn't sure how it had happened, but there seemed to be an understanding, a kind of camaraderie between them. It was almost as if they were becoming friends. It began with Karl, and spread in ways she couldn't explain even to herself. Shane didn't seem to think she was bad at relationships. Or perhaps he just didn't think it was so unusual to be bad at them. Why on earth that made her feel better, she didn't know. But as she walked away, she was fairly certain she'd set something right by coming here. She just wasn't altogether sure what, exactly.

By the time Tori unlocked the door of the third vacant office space, she and Caroline were both wilting. Switching on lights as she went, Tori said, "They need to keep the air-conditioning on if they want to lease these spaces. What do you think? Can you imagine yourself seeing clients here, providing it isn't a hundred and ten stifling degrees?"

Caroline took some time to consider that. The first two offices had been renovated twenty years ago, this one within the past five. The drop ceilings were probably good for acoustics, as was the commercial-grade carpeting beneath her feet. She supposed she could have set up an office here, but the space could have housed an insurance office or a Baby Gap just as easily. "It seems awfully generic," Caroline said.

"I thought you'd say that."

The last door Tori opened led to a narrow back alley paved in old bricks. The buildings lining the alley were covered in vines stirring on a marvelous breeze. Tori and Caroline were silent for a moment, appreciating the relief from the oppressive heat.

"That must have special meaning," Tori said.

Caroline hadn't realized she was tracing the edges of her charm. "It was my mother's."

"What is it?" Tori asked, taking it between her thumb and index finger.

"It's whatever you want it to be. My mother found it in the dirt on a narrow little street in Seville on her honeymoon. It's a dollop of pewter she thought looked like an abstract heart. My father had it made into a charm for her. My grandfather said she never took it off. I've always wondered why she wasn't wearing it when the plane crashed."

"You said she died when you were small?"

She nodded. "I found it in the bottom of a large box my grandfather brought to my room my first summer with him."

The bangles on Tori's wrists jangled slightly as she released the charm. Inhaling something sweet on the warm air, Caroline spied a honeysuckle vine growing up the side of the building. The pale yellow flowers were a perfect match for the blond streaks in Tori's hair, and the scent was synonymous with her bold sweetness. On that day when Caroline's grandfather had placed the box of her parents' things on her bed, it had been raining outside, and the air had been heavy with the scent of rain-drenched wild roses on the trellis outside her bedroom window. Until this moment, Caroline hadn't realized she associated scents with particular events and experiences in her life.

"It must have been hard on your grandfather, losing his daughter that way, and suddenly finding himself parenting again. What did he say?"

"He didn't say anything. He removed his glasses, took an old-fashioned handkerchief from his pocket and dried his eyes."

Caroline remembered it so clearly. For the

143

first eight years of her life, she'd been a carefree little girl who took for granted that she was the center of the universe. Her parents had been young. Her grandfather was old. She recalled making the distinction. She'd loved him with her whole heart, and she was so thankful to have him, to have somebody. Watching him dry his eyes that day, she'd vowed to cause him as little worry and grief as possible.

"Subconsciously I think I've been looking for a man like my grandfather ever since."

"At least we won't be competing for the same guys. You can hold out for the saints and I'll take the sinners."

Caroline never knew what Tori was going to say. "You like sinners?"

"Not abusers or criminals or creepy guys, but I prefer guys who are at least as bad as I am."

While Caroline was wondering about that, Tori led the way back through the building. After making sure everything was locked up tight, she said, "What else was in the box that day?"

They fell into step, starting toward the realty office a few blocks away. "My father's watch and some framed pictures and photo albums. My father was an amateur photographer, and my mom and I were his favorite subjects. Every time I looked at them that summer, I cried and cried. The hardest part was coming to the end where there were pages left unfilled. A psychiatrist would probably say I began compartmentalizing my life the day I put them away. Lately, I've been allowing myself to imagine how different my life might have been if my parents' plane hadn't crashed." Caroline placed a hand over her little paunch. "I want more for my child. Someday, when my baby is old enough, I'll tell him or her all the stories that make up our family history."

"Do it before he's fifteen. Or it'll be too late."

They reached the realty office in silence. Before Tori went inside and Caroline unlocked her car, she said, "Does Andy know how often you think of him, how much you love him?"

Tori looked straight ahead.

"Don't give up on him, Tori. I have to believe that when it comes to our children, it's never too late."

Andy's back was to Tori, but she could tell from the tenseness in his shoulders that he'd heard her. He pretended to look out the window. He got a bag of chips out of the pantry. He reset the clock on the microwave.

That thing was always off.

Eventually he ran out of diversions, but he still didn't look at her.

"Come on, Andy. Where would you like to go. Europe? Spain? How about Vegas?"

"Yeah, right, Mom."

She was trying to entice him to take a vacation with her. Most kids would jump at the chance to go to Vegas, and Europe; oh, she would have been dancing around the room at the prospect. "It's summer. Your dad would give you the time off."

He was shaking his head before he'd given it any thought.

Accepting that, she tried a different tack. "It seems like we never see each other anymore."

"I'm here all the time."

In your room, she wanted to say. In your own sad silent world.

"You're dressed up. You going out?"

He still wasn't looking at her, which made the observation all the more telling. "I don't have to. We could go somewhere. Are you hungry? Or we could take in a movie. I know guys your age don't want to be seen with their mothers. We could go to Traverse City where nobody would know us."

"It's Friday night," he said. "I'm riding my bike to Dad's."

"I could drop you off there later. Hey, we could invite one of your classmates to go with us."

She knew she'd said the wrong thing the minute it left her lips. Andy drew himself up to his full height, and yet he seemed to retreat before her eyes. Taking a water bottle from the refrigerator, he mumbled a good-bye of sorts.

She knew he was mad. But he never raised his voice. Most of the time she had to go in search of him to see if he was even home. The only sign that he was gone now was the quiet click the door made as it closed.

When it comes to our children, we can't give up.

Yeah, right, Tori thought. Caroline had meant well, but she didn't know shit about Andy's problems. Nobody knew how deep this rift went. Except Tori and Andy.

She wandered aimlessly through her house. She didn't know how Andy stood the silence. She hated it. She always had. She needed people, noise, action, excitement, anything but silence. Pattie would be busy with Dave and the kids, but Tori considered calling Nell or Elaine or Caroline.

Her reflection in the mirror across the living room startled her. Damn, she looked good. Sometimes she forgot just how good.

Wetting her lips, she smiled demurely at her image, imagining that some attractive man was smiling back. The girls were great. They were fantastic. If she needed a shoulder to cry on, an ear to bend, or unconditional acceptance, she would call them. But she needed something they couldn't give her. She needed to see that first spark of interest in a man's eyes, needed to feel strong arms around her, and to know someone thought she was beautiful, even if she knew the truth.

She forced the need down for now. But she knew it was only a matter of time.

CHAPTER 9

Caroline was becoming accustomed to the scent of disinfectant and stale breath that permeated the manor, as the staff and residents call it. It hadn't made her queasy in a week. Other than a brief episode of morning sickness every day upon arising, she felt wonderful. It was Tuesday. She hadn't heard from Tori since Friday when they'd looked at those vacant office spaces. Caroline wanted to talk to her, but so far, their only communication had been through voice mail.

Caroline took long walks every day. She read voraciously and indulged in an occasional nap. And every day she visited Karl.

She'd found that if she arrived in the morning, he was more alert. True to form today, he was awake when she entered his room. As he had each day this past week, he waited to smile until after he introduced himself.

She accepted the handshake. Inside, she felt a pang of disappointment because he didn't know they were family. Still, she arrived every morning at ten, and every morning she asked, "Shall we find some sunshine, Karl?"

As always, he gave the invitation some thought before accepting, and after a shaky rise to his feet, he began the long walk, steadying himself with his cane. Many of the other men wore knit pants with elastic waists. Most shuffled through their days in their bedroom slippers. Karl dressed every day in old but freshly laundered slacks and pressed, buttoned shirts. His shoes and belt were old leather, his hair sparse and white, his hands age-spotted. He was a nice-looking old gentleman, and undoubtedly had been a handsome devil in his youth. Caroline hadn't planned to feel such tender affection for him.

He always tired halfway into his walk to the courtyard. With quiet dignity, he accepted a ride in the wheelchair she pushed. She spoke to several residents and staff along the way, but Karl said nothing until he reached their destination, and then only after she spread the quilt on the ground near his chair in the dappled shade of a flowering crab-apple tree.

"Tea, Karl?" she asked, taking a Thermos and two teacups from her woven bag.

"Only if it's Earl Grey."

The brew steamed as she poured. And every morning as she watched him take that first sip, she felt a sense of wonder, for Earl Grey had been her grandfather's favorite tea, too. Her *other* grandfather's. She wondered if Henry had thought of Karl often through the years, and vice versa. Had Karl known that Anna died young? Caroline had so many questions. She'd tried asking a few of them a few days ago, but they'd only confused and frustrated Karl. She hadn't brought them up again.

"Are you my new secretary?" His voice was raspy and his finger shook slightly as he pointed at the legal pad she'd been using to take notes of his stories.

"Actually, I was an attorney in Chicago for twelve years. I'm thinking about opening a law office here in Harbor Woods."

"You'll want to look into reciprocity between Michigan and Illinois. I imagine there's an exorbitant fee, but it would be more efficient to waive into the Michigan State Bar than to take the exam again."

Caroline stared at the old man. Reciprocity was a term used by attorneys. "How did you know that?"

151

He looked at her blankly. "How did I know what?"

"How did you know about reciprocity between states?"

"Rep what?"

She was adjusting to the way Karl's mind worked. He could recall in vivid detail events that had happened ten, fifty, even seventy-five years ago, but couldn't recall something he'd told her moments earlier. One of the kindly aides compared an aging mind to the intricate workings of a clock whose gears slipped. "Sometimes," the other woman had said, "everything lines up, and the clock strikes the proper hour, but most of the time you get something else entirely. There's a delicate beauty in the rhythm of it, if you look for it."

Caroline was learning to look for it.

She was also learning to take each day as it came. She enjoyed her morning visits with Karl. The residents whose rooms overlooked the courtyard kept bird feeders outside their windows. Flowers bloomed everywhere. Hummingbirds and finches and butterflies made the gardens home. Sitting in the sunshine on this warm July morning, Caroline was discovering a new way to understand, a new way to get to know a kindly, gentlemanly old soul.

"There's Shane," Karl said.

He was full of surprises today, but he was right. Looking over her shoulder, she saw Shane talking to a nurse on the other side of the courtyard.

"Do you know him?" Caroline asked, curious.

Karl sipped his tea thoughtfully. "I used to hear his parents yelling from my house. Sometimes they screamed at each other, sometimes at Shane. That boy was always into something. Once I went out to get an onion and fresh tomato from my garden, only to discover they'd all been pulled. All the carrots, too. Everything was laying on top of the ground, ruined. I knew right away who'd done it. He couldn't have been more than five or six years old, but Shane admitted to it right away. I didn't know what to do with him. It was either take him over my knee or take him fishing. Ever since then, fishing's all he wants to do. Haven't known a moment's peace since, but at least my garden thrives."

Caroline laughed.

"What's so funny?"

"Nothing," she said. "Everything." Looking into Karl's watery blue eyes, she sobered. "Life, I suppose."

■ ■ ■ ■

Caroline was a little surprised to see Shane waiting for her when she left the manor. He'd dropped in to say hello to Karl, but hadn't stayed. She'd thought he'd left the nursing home twenty minutes ago.

It wasn't even noon yet, and already the sun was so hot the asphalt parking lot felt soft beneath the soles of her shoes. The local meteorologist was calling it the first heat wave of the summer, and was predicting that it would last through the upcoming holiday weekend. The weather was big news here.

Shane was opening his car door when she reached her vehicle, which was parked next to his. This was the first time they'd spoken since she'd gone to the marina last week.

"I'm curious about something," she said. "I noticed books on Karl's bedside table. Does he like to read?"

Shane looked at her over the roof of his car. "No."

"But he used to?"

"Yes."

Sometimes talking to Shane felt like conducting a cross-examination. Despite that fact, understanding dawned. "So now you read to him," she said quietly.

He shrugged, something he often did when she came too close to something personal.

"What are you reading to him now?"

"*The Old Man And The Sea* is one of his favorites."

"He likes Hemingway?" she asked.

"A lot of people up here claim a connection to Hemingway, who spent summers near Horton Bay when he was a boy. If you want the locals to know you're a tourist, call it *Horton's* Bay."

"I'll take it under advisement."

He didn't get into his car. It was as if he had something on his mind. That, at least, wasn't surprising. She knew his situation, and the man had more than his fair share of problems. A little while ago she'd been picturing an urchin pulling up vegetables in his neighbor's garden. That urchin had grown into a man who read the classics to a dear old friend. "Karl's lucky to have you."

He shrugged.

"What did Karl do?" she asked. "For a living, I mean."

"He was a lawyer for forty-five years. I thought you knew that."

Caroline shook her head. "All I know is

what you and Karl, and Anna, have told me."

Shane nearly singed his arm where he attempted to rest it on the top of his car. Being careful not to touch the hot roof, he looked at Caroline over the top of it. Until now, he hadn't thought about how it would feel to have to make the kinds of discoveries she was making. He'd always known exactly where he came from. He knew his father had taken up with other women from time to time and that his mother drank too much. In the summertime when the windows were open, everyone on their street had known. Shane knew he resembled his uncle in Wisconsin, and he knew that if he needed anything, either his sister down in Baton Rouge or any one of his cousins would come through. He couldn't imagine *not* knowing those kinds of things.

"Do you think Karl ever guessed the reason Anna married his best friend?" she asked.

Sweat ran down the side of Shane's neck as he answered. "If I'd received a letter like that, I would have wondered." He thought about the care meeting he'd just had with Karl's doctor. During a recent examination, Dr. Anderson had noticed something unusual when he'd listened to Karl's heart.

The subsequent EKG had revealed a leaky valve. Time was running out for his old neighbor.

"Besides the letter," she said, "did you find anything else in the lighthouse?"

"Sixty years' worth of dust." He squinted as he looked at her, the hot breeze ruffling the collar of her shirt at her neck. "I searched the entire place, Caroline. That diary isn't there."

"That means that everything I'll ever learn about Karl will come in the form of the brief memories he shares over morning tea. He must have received that letter while he was in France, and yet he hid it in the lighthouse. I wonder why."

"Maybe he felt it belonged there."

"That's what Anna's first entry said, too, and yet it's not there."

"There is another place it might be," he said, then silently cussed himself out for opening his mouth.

"Where?" she asked.

"In Karl's house. Maybe he's the one who found it."

She wasn't asking anything of him. He could have gotten in his car and gotten the hell out of there. Instead, he heard himself say, "Would you care to conduct a little search sometime?"

He hadn't meant to offer. Caroline knew, because he practically bit through his cheek after asking. "When?" she asked.

"Lately I have a long list of things I'm not doing, but my to-do list is wide-open."

She wasn't surprised he wasn't going to let her live that down. "Imagine that. When?" she asked again.

"The week before the Fourth is always hell at the marina. How about next week. Tuesday?"

"Tuesday, it is."

He finally got in his car and drove away. He didn't look back. She knew, because she watched to see if he would, not that it would have mattered. His beard hid his expressions anyway. Perhaps that was why he wore it.

She didn't know what was wrong with her. Here she was, sweltering in a parking lot that smelled like hot tar, wearing the most unbecoming clothes she owned — she couldn't even zip up her pants all the way anymore. And she was wondering what Shane would look like in the middle of her bed, wearing nothing at all. Last night she'd cried while watching a movie. She never did that. The books assured her it was normal to be emotional right now, due to fluctuating hormone levels. She wondered if it could have anything to do with these fantasies. She didn't have any idea who to ask, which was fine, since she had no intention of acting on the fantasy anyway.

On Friday, Caroline watched the salesclerk ring up her purchases. The impeccably dressed woman looked extremely happy. She was probably working on commission.

"Didn't I tell you Auntie Tori would take care of everything?" Tori asked, nudging Caroline's shoulder with her own.

Eyeing the stack of clothes being placed carefully into bags with sturdy handles, Caroline said, "Remind me never to go shopping for maternity clothes with someone who looks like that."

The clerk smiled. Clearly, she wasn't buying this "Auntie Tori" business any more than Caroline was. That was nearly all Caroline hadn't bought.

Everything in the boutique had been designed by two sisters who, when pregnant themselves several years ago, had found that the fashions available at the time looked as if they came from a tent and awning shop. The sisters had decided to design their own line, and the pieces were fabulous.

Tori had an eye for fashion, and had helped Caroline select most of today's purchases. Some were fluid and were designed to conceal her growing waistline. Others were fitted and would accentuate it.

"Now," Tori said, helping Caroline carry the packages. "For the right shoes."

"Did you say shoes?"

Caroline reached the sidewalk, laughing.

Something was happening to her this summer. For most of her life she'd been dynamically focused and completely goal oriented. She'd had Maria and her grandfather and a few colleagues with whom she'd been friendly. Not one of those colleagues had contacted her since she'd left Chicago. It was as if she'd stepped off the face of the planet, fallen through the stratosphere, and had landed here in Harbor Woods. All because her grandfather hadn't thrown away a letter written long ago by the girl he'd loved and married.

"Do you believe in fate, Tori?" Caroline studied the other woman closely.

All morning she'd been trying to find a way to broach the subject of Shane. She and Tori had talked and they'd laughed and Tori had teased Caroline about her growing waistline, but there hadn't been an opening into which she could slip Shane's name casually. She didn't want to blurt it out, for doing so would make it seem as if there was more to the relationship than there was. Outside of one brief fantasy, there wasn't much to tell.

"I believe we create our own fate," Tori answered. "And I believe in shoes. Are you coming or aren't you?"

Caroline started to follow, only to pause, dizzy.

"Are you all right?" Tori asked.

The question took Caroline back to her grandfather's house in Lake Forest when she'd been sure she would explode if one more person asked her that. She no longer felt like exploding. And it wasn't difficult to breathe. She *was* light-headed, however. "I think it's this heat," she said. "Would you mind if we shop for shoes another time?"

"Do you need a ride?" Tori looked concerned.

Reaching for the bags Tori carried, Caroline said, "I think I'll slip into something cool, such as the restaurant on the corner, and have something cold to drink."

"In that case I'd better keep moving," Tori said. "Are you coming to girls' night tomorrow?"

"I wouldn't miss it."

They parted ways. The heat wave had continued, ringing in the busiest months of the summer. Tourists were everywhere, dressed so skimpily that much more than their noses were sunburned. Falling into step with the flow of pedestrians, Caroline started toward the corner restaurant. A sign in a storefront caught her attention. She stopped abruptly in the middle of the crowded sidewalk, forcing surprised shoppers to veer around her.

There on the window were the words Karl T. Peterson, Attorney-at-Law. The script was old-fashioned and professionally printed. Directly above it hung a faded red sign: For Sale or Lease.

Caroline had gone to the museum on Lake Shore Drive after visiting Karl today. The displays of coins, anchors and sunken artifacts were impressive, but the real treasures had been buried in the newspaper archives at the library on the corner of Third and Elm streets where she'd read a dozen articles about the town's formidable lawyer. Karl Peterson had sat on committees and boards, but more often than not, the grainy photographs had depicted him with the people he'd helped. In one photograph, he stood next to the parents of a slain girl, the father wrongly accused of the horrific crime. In another, he was leaving the courthouse with a poor farmer following a land dispute with the state, and in yet another he stood beside a woman victorious after a long battle to win custody of an ill child.

She'd earned a six-figure income for years, and yet she doubted she'd changed any of her former clients' lives in any lasting, meaningful way. Karl hadn't made a great deal of money, and yet he'd touched more lives than she knew.

Trying to keep from getting run over by window-shoppers, she shifted the bags into one hand and reached into her purse for a pen. After scribbling down the number, she stared at the name in the window. She'd looked at office space in Charlevoix. And here was Karl's former office, vacant, and right here in Harbor Woods.

More and more, Caroline was coming to believe in fate.

CHAPTER 10

For a long time, the only sounds in Elaine's grand living room were those the four massage therapists made as they worked their magic on the friends stretched out on portable massage tables evenly spaced down the center of the room. Nell, Elaine and Tori were lying on their stomachs on the padded tables, a sheet covering them from thigh to waist. Caroline was lying on her back, her pregnant stomach making it difficult for her to get more than a shoulder massage. Aromatic candles flickered throughout the room and mood music played from a technician's portable CD player.

"Oh, yeah," Tori said. "Right there."

Nell giggled. "Sorry," she told her technician. "That's a ticklish spot. If I forget to tell you later, thanks for tonight, Elaine. This is fabulous."

Caroline could only imagine how much it must have cost to hire four licensed, uniformed technicians for an entire Saturday evening of facials, manicures and massages.

"Don't thank me," Elaine said, getting comfortable. "Thank my lying, cheating, two-timing, ass-is-grass husband."

"Does Justin know you know, then?" Nell asked from the table next to her.

"He knows something is going on. He's been watching me closely, and yesterday he sent me two-dozen peach-colored roses, despite the fact that I pretended to be asleep when he wanted to have sex the night before. He's still seeing her."

"What are you going to do?" Nell asked.

"I don't know yet," Elaine said. "I'd like to talk to you about that, Caroline."

Silence.

"Caroline?"

Caroline was drifting too far off the table to reply. It felt wonderful to relax. She'd been keyed up since discovering that vacant office space yesterday. It wasn't uncommon for her to be impatient. It was just that in the past she'd always been able to use it to move things along. Standing on that sidewalk yesterday, pedestrians streaming past her, she'd known exactly what she wanted. And there was nothing she could do about it until the owner of that office space returned her call. Even Tori's hands were tied.

Caroline had spoken with someone at the State Bar Association, and had been assured that it was indeed possible, and in fact highly likely that she would be allowed to waive into the Michigan Bar, providing she supplied them with the proper information and it met with the review board's approval. That wasn't going to happen overnight, either.

She'd been dizzy again earlier while walking along the channel. Resting in the shade in a little park at the edge of Oval Lake, she'd seen Shane and his son. They were riding bikes, and had stopped to rest, too. Although Shane had introduced them, Andy had barely met her eyes. She understood why Shane and Tori worried.

"Caroline?"

"Yoo-hoo. Are you awake over there?" Elaine called.

"Barely," Caroline crooned softly.

"It's too bad Pattie couldn't join us," Nell said. "But she's spending the weekend with Dave and the kids."

"I guess I can forgive her for being happily married," Tori grumbled. "My ex is seeing someone."

Shane was seeing someone? Caroline thought.

"Who?" Nell and Elaine asked at the same time.

"I don't know, but I hear she's chunky. It figures. He never did appreciate everything I go through to look good."

Caroline digested the information. She remembered how alone Shane had looked that moment before he dove from the rock. No one should be that alone. The fact that he was involved didn't affect her one way or the other. She'd overreacted to simple human kindness. Still, if Shane was seeing someone, there was no sense mentioning their association to her friends.

She wondered who he was seeing.

Giving herself a mental shake, she lifted her head to look at Tori, only to lower it again dizzily. That was strange. She was light-headed again. She probably shouldn't have come. She'd felt better after resting in the shade by Oval Lake earlier. If they'd been planning anything other than the most decadently relaxing treat, she would have stayed home.

"You don't care, do you?" Nell asked. "I mean, you've been divorced for a long time."

"Why would I care?"

"Atta girl. Whose turn is it?" Nell asked.

Elaine and Tori groaned. Evidently, they went through this two or three times a year, when Nell asked everyone to suspend reality and visualize the life she wanted.

"Nell, this is the most lame pastime in the world. Aren't we a little old for what-if?" Elaine asked.

"Who are you calling old?" Tori said. "What do you want, Elaine? Come on. Nell's right. It never hurts to dream."

"Fine," Elaine grumbled. "I'd like to take Trish and Tracy to Rome and never return. And while I'm there, I'd like a piano to fall on Justin's mistress. And I'd like Justin to experience what I'm feeling. And if that isn't possible, I wish he'd get his johnson stuck in his zipper and have to have it surgically removed."

"The zipper or his johnson?" Nell asked.

Everyone chuckled. Even the massage technicians.

"He deserves worse," Nell said. "But for someone who didn't want to play, that's a lot of wishes. You're next, Caroline. What do you want?"

"My wish doesn't involve pianos or zippers."

"Count your blessings," Elaine mumbled.

"I want to open a law practice in Harbor Woods. And I would appreciate it if Logan and Bernice Carlson would return my call. Who puts a For Sale sign in a window then doesn't have the decency to return a simple phone call? Okay, ten simple phone calls."

"They'll call. Who's next?" Tori asked.

The technicians continued kneading and massaging. In the center of the room, Nell said, "I want to lose twenty more pounds, and I'd like to do it eating hot fudge sundaes. Your turn, Tori. What do you want?"

"I want to experience the breathless wonder of anticipation of a girl at her first dance."

Caroline, Nell and Elaine all raised their heads to look at her.

"Just making sure you're listening. What I really want is hot, blazing, mind-altering, ravenous sex." Eyeing the other three, she said, "Don't tell me you don't want the same thing."

Caroline wasn't certain Nell's latest giggle was due to another ticklish spot.

"It isn't too late to change your wishes," Tori cajoled. "Oh," she said around a deep moan. "I have one more wish. I'd like breast implants, too."

Even the massage therapists groaned.

By the time the massages were over, everyone felt sluggish. Caroline dressed in the hall bathroom. Taking a moment to splash her face with cool water, she studied her reflection in the mirror. Her skin was glowing from the facial, her nails beautiful from the manicure, her muscles relaxed at last. Her light-headedness had finally passed.

The entrepreneurs had taken their tables, candles and mood music, and gone. Feeling much better, Caroline left the bathroom, intent upon joining her friends in the living room.

She didn't make it far before the wooziness returned.

Caroline stopped in her tracks, placing a steadying hand on the wall. Lights flashed before her eyes.

"What's wrong?" Nell, the group nurturer, asked.

"Caroline?"

Tori's voice came from far away.

"Something's wrong with her."

"She's pale as a ghost."

"Sit down, Caroline. Now."

Caroline blinked. "I think I moved too fast. I just felt — something."

"What?" Elaine said, rising quickly from the sofa.

"I think I'm going to —" Caroline took another step. But only one.

■ ■ ■ ■

"She's coming to."

"There you are."

"Can you hear me?"

Caroline stared up into three familiar faces, one narrow, one round, one nearly perfect, all etched with concern. "Why am I on the floor?"

"You fainted."

"I did?"

"Don't you remember?"

"How many fingers am I holding up?"

"She didn't hit her head, Nell," Tori insisted.

"Do you have a better suggestion?" Nell grumbled.

"I've been feeling strange today," Caroline said groggily.

"Strange, how?"

"Light-headed."

"All day?" Elaine asked.

Caroline rolled to her side. The moment she sat up, noise roared through her ears. She quickly lay down again.

"What should we do?" Elaine asked.

"I don't know."

"I think we should take her to the emergency room," Nell said.

"That isn't necessary," Caroline said weakly.

"She is pregnant," Elaine continued as if Caroline weren't there.

"And over forty," Nell said. "Sorry, Caroline."

"Elaine," Tori called, taking charge. "Go unlock your van. Nell, help me get Caroline to her feet. Oomph. Geez, Caroline, for a size six, you weigh a ton. Where's a man when you need one?"

Caroline accepted the help getting situated in the back seat of Elaine's van, with the cool washcloth Nell placed on her forehead and the pillow Tori tucked behind her head. Since she knew it was futile to argue, she let all of them fuss over her and ask how she was feeling every fifteen-and-a-half seconds. At some time during the short drive to the hospital, she realized something she hadn't known about friendship. Sometimes, the doting was more for the doters' benefit than the dotee.

It didn't take long to reach County General. Elaine parked beneath the portico and Nell ran for a wheelchair. Together, she and Tori pushed Caroline in.

The emergency room was noisy. Phones rang, a toddler cried, and those waiting complained about how long it was taking.

The nurse who took Caroline's vitals insisted a bee sting, two sprained ankles, several serious sunburns, an ear infection, a possible food poisoning, a finger pierced by a fish hook and two men complaining of chest pains were par for the course on any holiday weekend. Being pregnant had moved Caroline to near the top of the waiting list. A thermometer had been stuck in her mouth. As a precautionary measure, the midwife had been called.

The curtain was drawn around Caroline's bed, for all the good it did. Nell, Elaine and Tori crowded around as the midwife listened to Caroline's heartbeat.

"She said she's been light-headed all day."

"Yesterday, too."

"She went out walking in this heat."

"Do you think it's heatstroke?"

Along with some very impressive credentials as a nurse-practitioner and midwife, Alice Cavanaugh possessed the rare and uncanny ability to move her eyebrows independently of each other. She demonstrated while casting a pointed look at the other three women.

Taking the hint, Elaine, Nell and Tori shut up.

Once again, Alice turned her attention to the patient. "Have you fainted before?"

"No." Caroline's voice sounded small. "Is my baby all right?"

The midwife placed her stethoscope on Caroline's belly. "Your baby has a strong heartbeat. And you're not spotting. Those are good signs."

Thank God for good signs. Caroline started to relax.

"Tell me what happened," the midwife said.

"I felt light-headed earlier, but I assumed it was the heat."

"It's possible it was."

"After my friends and I had facials and massages tonight, I felt much better. In fact, I thought the bout had passed completely, when I felt something."

"Something," Alice repeated.

Caroline nodded. "Wait. There it is again."

"What is it?" Nell asked. "See? I was afraid something was wrong."

"I felt this just before I fainted. In my excitement, I moved a little too fast."

"Are you in pain?" Tori asked.

"Where does it hurt?" Elaine quipped.

"Shouldn't she be lying flat?" Nell insisted.

When the midwife was able to get a word in edgewise, she said, "What did you feel, Caroline?"

"Like something nudged me. From the inside."

"That's what you felt?" Nell asked.

"That's why you fainted?" Elaine said.

"Why didn't you say so?" Tori complained.

Again, the other three women all talked at once.

"We rushed you to the emergency room because your baby moved?" Elaine grumbled.

Caroline didn't have the heart to remind everyone that coming to the hospital hadn't been her idea. She was too busy feeling awestruck by the knowledge that she'd felt her baby.

She'd felt life, her child's life.

"Everybody except Caroline, out," Alice Cavanaugh ordered.

"We can't leave."

"Out."

"We're her support group."

"Out!"

"We're going. We're going. There's no need to yell." Tori threaded her arm through Nell's.

Elaine was sensible enough to follow on her own.

When the curtain stopped fluttering again, the midwife said, "Just to be on the safe side, I want to run a few tests, do a complete blood workup, and schedule an ultrasound. You didn't faint because the baby moved. You and the baby are probably fine, but I want to ensure you stay that way. The bad news is, your friends probably won't let you live this down."

Caroline nodded. She'd fainted, but she was feeling better now. She wasn't worried about Tori, Nell and Elaine. "They mean well," she said. "Besides, I can handle my friends."

It felt good to say it. It felt even better to have friends who cared.

"Now," she said, looking the midwife in the eye, "tell me about these tests you want to order. What are you looking for?" She placed her hand over her abdomen. "What do I need to watch for? You're sure my baby's heartbeat is strong?"

Alice Cavanaugh outlined the tests she was ordering, their purpose, and the reasons she was taking these precautions. Before releasing Caroline to her friends, she placed the stethoscope to Caroline's belly again, letting Caroline listen to the strong, steady, and amazingly loud heartbeat of her child.

Caroline told Tori, Nell and Elaine all about it during the drive back to her summerhouse. She couldn't seem to stop smiling. As she let herself into her house, her baby was no longer some abstract notion. Her child had a heartbeat. He or she was real. And Caroline didn't think she would ever be the same again.

Oh, she hoped not.

Tori wandered through her house in Charlevoix. The air-conditioning was on but even with the windows closed, she heard the occasional *pop-pop-pop* of fireworks over Lake Charlevoix. The big fireworks extravaganza over Lake Michigan wouldn't take place until tomorrow night.

It was the Fourth of July weekend, the biggest party weekend of the summer. And she was wandering through her house. At eleven o'clock. Alone.

She was trying not to feel sorry for herself. She and the girls had planned to go to a club after their massages and facials. Caroline had agreed to be their designated driver. Tori couldn't blame Caroline for bowing out following her scare earlier. Elaine and Nell hadn't wanted to go out after that, either.

It would have been good for both of them to go, but after leaving the hospital and dropping Caroline at her summerhouse, all they'd wanted to do was reminisce about their pregnancies and simpler times.

No matter how far women had come, there were two things in life that never ceased to turn the majority of them to mush: pregnancies and newborn babies. Maybe there were three, but damn, Tori hated to admit that men were on the list.

Nell had invited Tori to spend the evening with her and Elaine, but there was only so much reminiscing about childbirth Tori could take. She remembered her pregnancy. She'd only gained nineteen pounds, and wore her regular jeans home from the hospital. Not her skinny jeans, but jeans nonetheless. She'd started exercising four weeks later. She'd put Andy in his little snuggly seat and sat him in front of her while she worked out. He'd hardly squawked, watching her movements, mesmerized.

She'd been just as mesmerized with him.

Surely no woman had ever delivered a more beautiful child. At twenty-two, she'd practically been a baby herself. When she'd found out she was pregnant, she'd been terrified her life was over, that a baby would change everything. It hadn't been that way at all. She'd loved Andy from the moment she saw him. The intensity of her emotions had surprised her, and she remembered thinking that everything might just work out after all, which was extremely optimistic, especially for her, for she'd always bored easily.

She'd never tired of watching Andy grow. To this day, she loved him more than she loved another soul on earth.

Tori sighed. She supposed she shouldn't be surprised she'd wound up on this side of the living room. It was where she kept the albums and photographs. She picked up the one family photo she'd kept out after the divorce.

Her hair had been shorter then. And look at that nose! She shuddered. But then she looked at the family she, Shane and Andy had been. They'd been beautiful, her old nose not withstanding: an above-average attractive couple and their adorable seven-year-old son.

Andy *had* been adorable. She'd bought his chinos and that little shirt with the anchors on it in Traverse City. No amount of hair gel had tamed that little cowlick. She could practically hear his high-pitched, little-boy laughter. She couldn't believe how much she missed it.

He was looking at his father in the picture. He'd adored Shane. He still did. Back then, they'd both adored her, too. In the end, it had been the man she'd grown bored with, the man she'd blamed for her unhappiness. And now he was seeing someone else.

"A chunky redhead," Andy had said.

That wasn't the reason for this niggling fear, this quiet panic. She wanted to believe she was better than that. She was worried about Andy. She was so weary of worrying. He was wounded so deeply she couldn't reach him anymore. What if he never recovered?

Guilt and worry churned inside her. She felt wretched. The need was back, stronger. Times like these, she wished she was in a relationship. A little slow dancing, a man's strong arms, and later . . .

Ah, yes, later was what she needed most of all.

She knew how she looked these days. Perhaps she wasn't drop-dead gorgeous, but she was close. Men always noticed her when she entered a room. And it wasn't just the streaks in her hair, her perfect nose and sexy shoes. Nell insisted Tori emitted pheromones.

Too bad Nell and Elaine hadn't wanted to go to the club. Tori needed a diversion tonight. She was only thirty-seven years old, and everyone knew women peaked in their thirties. There was nothing wrong with wanting a diversion. What better diversion was there than a man who couldn't take his eyes off her, who only saw what was on the outside?

A man who couldn't see the real her.

Her wandering took her to the hallway. She'd bought this house shortly after the divorce. She was proud that she'd been able to afford it on her own. It wasn't large, but it was beautifully decorated. And it was hers.

Her bedroom was on the right, Andy's on the left. His door was closed partway. The light was off. It was Saturday night, a holiday weekend, and her son had gone to bed at nine-thirty.

Pushing the door open a little farther, she called his name softly. Listening, she tiptoed to his bed. His breathing was deep and even. Moonlight spilled across his pillow, allowing her to make out the shape of his face and the bony shoulder not covered by the sheet. His face and arms were tan, but the rest of him was so pale. He never took his shirt off, never tried to impress the girls or the guys. He never seemed to have any fun.

Emotion welled in her chest, in her throat, behind her eyes. He looked painfully serious, even in sleep.

He never laughed anymore. He hardly talked to her. He spent time with his father nearly every day now. It was as if *she* was the enemy. She knew he blamed her for the divorce. He was depressed, lost, sad.

But he was no dummy.

He never went out with friends anymore. His father thought they needed to give him more time. He needed a goddamned shrink. That was what he needed.

Her son was more like her than she wanted him to be.

She left his room, leaving his door the way she'd found it. Now what? The thought of whiling away a festive holiday weekend night alone was almost more than she could bear. She wanted life, noise, excitement, fun. If only Nell and Elaine hadn't bailed on her.

So what if they had? a voice in the back of her mind whispered.

Sure, it would have been nice to go to the club with friends. But she was a big girl. More importantly, she was a grown woman, a grown woman with needs, and tonight those needs wouldn't be tamped down.

She scribbled a note for Andy — not that he ever woke up once he was asleep. She left it on the refrigerator, just in case, then dashed into her bedroom for her lipstick and i.d.

CHAPTER 11

Caroline took a Thermos and two teacups from her large woven bag. "Tea, Karl?"

Every day for two weeks Karl had answered in the same manner. Today, he said nothing. He was listless this morning. He'd tired sooner than usual, and had ridden in his wheelchair most of the way to the courtyard.

"Would you care for a cup of tea?" Caroline repeated gently.

He coughed. When he was able to speak, he said, "If it's Earl Grey."

"Did the fireworks keep you awake last night?" she asked, pouring the steaming brew.

"Fireworks?"

He coughed again, and she could see how much it cost him. Handing him his tea, she wondered if it was going to be one of those rare visits in which she did most of the talking.

"You were right about reciprocity between the Illinois and Michigan State Bar Associations, Karl. I've started the process, provided them with the proper affidavit and forms and submitted my work history. You'll never guess where I'd like to set up my new practice."

Karl sipped his tea quietly.

Continuing as if he were participating in the conversation, she said, "There's an office space available on Main Street right here in Harbor Woods. It's where you practiced law, isn't it?"

"Henry and I planned to start a practice there together."

Caroline held her breath. "Henry?" she whispered.

"My buddy and I. Went to school together. His family was better off than mine. It didn't bother Henry or me."

He paused, and Caroline feared that was all he would say. It was a relief when he continued.

"People always thought I was the bigger hellion. Wasn't true. He just never got caught." Karl coughed into an old-fashioned handkerchief. Folding it carefully and returning it to his pocket, he said, "One time we climbed to the top of the water tower after dark and wrote something

184

scandalous about the teacher. Henry did half the writing, but I'm the one who got caught with green paint on my hands. Took a whipping from the teacher for it, and then another one from my father when he found out."

"Did Henry get spanked, too?"

"No."

"Why?" she asked.

"Nobody knew."

"You didn't tell anybody you had an accomplice?" she asked.

"He would have done the same for me."

Caroline wondered if Karl would say that if his memories hadn't stopped there, if he'd gone on to recall the last letter he'd received from Anna, and what must have felt like the ultimate betrayal.

Karl finished the rest of his tea in silence. Taking his empty cup and saucer from him, she turned slightly, her head bowed as she placed the dishes in her bag near Karl's chair. Something brushed her hair. At first she thought it was the warm breeze, so soft, so tentative was the touch. Being careful to move slowly, she looked up from her position on the quilt, into Karl's faded blue eyes.

His hand stilled in midair. He looked startled, as if he was expecting her to be someone else.

"Whatever happened to Henry?" she asked quietly.

He made no reply.

Caroline thought about the diary she and Shane were going to look for later this evening. Had Karl discovered Anna's hiding place in the lighthouse? Had he read it, then put it away someplace safe?

Had Karl and Henry ever spoken again? Had Karl tried to find Anna when he returned home after the war? Or had it all been over, in the past but not forgotten? There were a hundred questions she wanted to ask him, a hundred memories she wanted to share with him about her life with the man who had raised her. But she didn't want to upset him, nor was it her place to defend Henry O'Shaughnessy, not to Karl, not after all this time, so she simply returned Karl's gentle smile and told herself to be happy with the one thing she'd been granted.

Time.

There was something sad about a house that had sustained someone's existence for a very long time but now sat empty.

It was Tuesday evening, and Caroline and Shane had already made a quick pass through Karl's house at 408 Prospect Street.

186

Like the man who'd lived there, his home was unpretentious, uncluttered and unimposing. Cape Cod in style, it had two bedrooms downstairs and one up. Inexpensive framed prints of lighthouses and ships hung in every room. There were only a few personal photographs. One was a black-and-white picture of a man and woman. Caroline assumed they were Karl's parents, her great-grandparents. She stared at the photo for a long time. Next to it was a photograph of a boy and a girl. She recognized Karl from his stance and mischievous grin. The little girl must have been his sister, Dolores. The only other frame on the low shelf contained a color snapshot of Shane and Karl. In their hands they each held a massive fish.

"I can't imagine sitting in a boat all day trying to catch one of these."

"You've never been fishing?" he asked.

"No."

"You haven't lived."

With a small smile, she said, "Of course, I've never dived off a cliff, either. Suffice to say I've never been what you would call a risk taker. Discovering I was pregnant has been a huge step for me."

"You never mention the father."

The scrape of a drawer being opened put

her in mind of fingernails on a chalkboard. Or perhaps that was the scrape of her conscience. "He's a brilliant litigation consultant, and the last I knew, he was thrilled to be reconciling with his ex-wife and two young sons. I think he would have viewed my little bombshell as a complication none of them needed."

"You *think?*"

Caroline grappled with what was morally and ethically right. More than anything, she needed to do what was best for her baby. She was doing the right thing, wasn't she?

She opened a drawer, too. Being careful not to disrupt anything, she looked inside. It reminded her that keeping secrets had far-reaching consequences. She was discovering many parallels between her situation and Anna's.

"I'm following my instincts. And I'm trying to do what's best for my child. How do people know for sure what that is?"

"Most of the time, we don't know," he said. "We do what we hope is best, and if we're lucky, every once in a while we get a glimmer in the form of a report card or an overheard telephone conversation or a smile that tells us we're on the right track."

There was something Caroline had noticed about parenthood. It united people in a way she'd never fathomed. It seemed to her that every parent wanted what was best for his or her child. And not one of them seemed to know for sure what that was. They were all flying blind.

And to think she'd almost missed it.

She opened another drawer, then quietly closed it again. Karl's house was adequately but rather meagerly furnished. The most impressive feature was his collection of books lining the floor-to-ceiling shelves in the living room. Volumes of Yeats, Hemingway and Angelou shared space with Grisham and Greeley, as well as entire shelves filled with law books and tomes whose authors she didn't recognize.

She pictured Karl standing where she was standing, choosing a book from his collection. "It doesn't feel right to be snooping through Karl's personal belongings."

"I thought you wanted to find your grandmother's diary."

"I do. At least I did."

Shane was staring at her.

"What?" she said.

"You're refreshing, that's all."

"*Refreshing* isn't a word normally used to describe me."

"That's a crying shame."

There was absolutely no reason to feel

sideswiped by the compliment. Shane Grady was good-looking, but there was nothing unusual about the cut of his dark hair or the breadth of his shoulders. It was just that sometimes, when he looked at her the way he was looking at her right now, she thought that perhaps she'd been looking for the wrong kind of man. Now why on earth should that surprise her? Everything else she'd thought was true was turning out to be false.

He thought she was refreshing.

She wondered who Shane was seeing, and if it was serious. She was tempted to say something coy, something like *You probably say that to a lot of women.*

She brought herself up short. Caroline Moore was not coy and she wouldn't pretend to be. She would either ask outright, or she wouldn't ask at all.

"Shane, are you in there?" A woman with a three-packs-a-day rasp called through the screen.

Shane swore under his breath. "Come on in, Mom," he said.

"What are you doing driving a Mercedes? You're coming up in the world."

Caroline recognized the large-boned woman shuffling inside. They'd spoken that morning shortly after her arrival in Harbor

Woods a month ago.

Letting the door slam shut behind her, Shane's mother stopped the moment she saw Caroline. "I see you found him."

"He was at the marina," Caroline said, introducing a smile into the conversation. "He was exactly where you said he would be. Hello, Mrs. Grady."

"Misses schmisses. My name's Rita. And it's Cooper. Not Grady. Took my maiden name back as soon as I gave Shane's old man the boot. Best way known to woman-kind to get in the last jab." She looked at her son. "What are you two doing over here, anyway?" She made a point of looking at Caroline's slightly rounded belly. "Holy mother, are you pregnant?"

"Mom."

"I, that is, yes, I am."

"Is it Shane's?"

"Mom!"

Caroline held up one hand to Shane. "It's all right." And to his mother, she said, "No, it isn't."

"Then why are you hiding over here?" Rita asked her son.

"We're not —" Shane didn't bother finishing.

"Have it your way. You always did like it better here than at home. Tell Andy to come see his Gram-maw-maw. My lawn needs mowing." She let the door bounce closed as she shuffled down the porch steps.

After several seconds, Shane said, "They claimed she would be nicer after she stopped drinking. They lied."

If Caroline didn't burn in hell for keeping her pregnancy from Phillip, chances were she wouldn't from laughing out loud now. She looked up at Shane. There were lines beside his eyes and between them. He wasn't a man whose life lacked worry. He was becoming easier and easier to be around.

"Would you care to get out of here?" he asked.

Glancing around Karl's house, she thought it sounded like a good idea. Perhaps too good an idea. She was doing her darnedest to come up with an alternate plan when it occurred to her that she was doing it again. She was compartmentalizing her life, ignoring her instincts and pretending they didn't matter.

Assuming her best courtroom stance, she looked at Shane and said, "Before we leave here, is there something you'd care to tell me?"

He exhaled loudly. He ran a hand through his hair. He finally looked at her and said,

"Did one of the nurses say something?"

One of the nurses? Caroline could only shake her head.

"You probably noticed Karl doesn't care to go to the courtyard anymore," he said.

Of course she'd noticed, but she didn't know what Karl had to do with her question.

"I spoke with his doctors a few days ago. He's losing ground, Caroline."

She lowered herself to a chair.

As Shane told her about the results of Karl's EKG and the prognosis, she traced her mother's charm with her fingertip. Speaking around the ache in her throat, she said, "Did the doctor say how long he has?"

"A few months at the most."

Before her throat closed up entirely, she heard herself say, "I thought you were going to say something else. I was prepared for that."

"What did you think I was going to tell you?"

She really didn't like this habit she'd developed for saying what she was thinking, but she replied, "I thought you were going to tell me you're seeing someone."

"Me?" His eyes were brown and clear and slightly bemused. "Put me in a scratchy robe and I could be a monk."

A monk, hmm? she thought as he locked the door and they went their separate ways. He certainly had the sandals and beard for it.

"The kid has your chin."

Caroline leaned closer to the ultrasound image in Tori's hand. "Where do you see a chin?"

The weather had finally broken, and a high-pressure system was to thank for the comfortable seventy-eight degrees. Caroline smiled, because Henry would have been pleased to see that she was taking an interest in the weather.

All five of the girls were having lunch at an outdoor table at a quaint Italian bistro in downtown Harbor Woods. They were celebrating the official signing of Caroline's new lease. The owners had finally called, and Caroline had agreed to rent the office space. Tori had added a rider, giving Caroline the option to buy. Soon, Karl's former offices would house her new practice.

The sonogram being passed around the table was icing on the cake. Caroline had memorized every facet of the image depicted on the film. She was five months along, and her baby was amazingly, perfectly formed. A tiny hand covered the lower half of his or her face, which meant Tori was joking about the likeness in chins.

The test results were back. Caroline was healthy, and by all accounts, so was her child. She had strict instructions to be careful, though, to take it easy and not overdo. Alice Cavanaugh continued to watch the levels of various components in her blood. Because Caroline had been on the pill when she'd conceived, an accurate due date had been elusive. However, judging from the size and development of the baby, they were fairly certain the pregnancy would reach full term by the second week in November.

"Did they say whether it's a boy or a girl?" Nell asked, staring at the sonogram.

"Alice is pretty sure she knows, but I want to be surprised. So far, the entire concept has been a surprise. Why stop now? I can hardly believe this is all happening, and yet I can't imagine going back to the way my life was before."

The fringe on the umbrella over their table swirled in the breeze like legs in a chorus line. A busboy chased away a bothersome seagull, and Tori smiled demurely at their waiter.

The man smiled back, then asked Elaine if she was ready to order. Elaine requested fresh-baked whitefish and steamed vegetables.

"Are you dieting, too?" Pattie asked.

Elaine started guiltily. "It never hurts to look one's best."

Which may or may not have meant she was going to give Justin the boot and move on to a more peaceful life, or at least one in which she was respected. At this point, Caroline couldn't be sure what Elaine was going to do.

Pattie said, "Make mine the same. And keep the coffee coming, would you?" She glanced at the others. "Molly kept the whole house awake most of the night. She had another earache."

Handing the waiter her menu, Caroline said, "I think I'd like the salmon with cucumber sauce and a glass of skim milk, please." She shrugged. "I'm supposed to eat more calcium."

Nell was next. "I'll have the baked lasagna and a side of fettuccine Alfredo and also stuffed manicotti. Screw this diet. I'm starving."

The waiter came to Tori again. "And what would you like?"

When she looked him up and down suggestively, Pattie nudged Elaine, who nudged Nell. Caroline was already watching the

196

silent exchange.

Easing her hair behind her shoulder in a manner that made every ring on her finger flash, Tori said, "I'll have the spinach fettuccine and a glass of your best chardonnay."

He didn't write it down. And he didn't leave.

"Why did you take my order last?" she asked.

"You seem like the kind of woman who appreciates prolonging a good thing."

The man was older than the average area waiters, which meant he was out of college. Actually, he looked thirtyish, and didn't seem any more self-conscious about the steamy undercurrents than Tori did. "Would you care for anything else?" he asked.

"I'll let you know." She smiled.

The minute he left the table, Nell said, "How do you do that?"

"Do what?"

Pattie said, "I was waiting for him to ask you if you were ordering the spinach because you were saving the meat for later."

Caroline almost choked on her ice water.

Pushing her bangs to one side, Elaine said, "Are you going to leave your number on the check?"

Tori shook her head.

"Why not?" three out of the other four

said at once.

"I'm pretty much sated."

They all leaned ahead, elbows resting on the table.

"You've met someone?" Elaine asked.

"You might say that."

"Are you going to see him again?" This time it was Nell who voiced everyone's question.

"I'm not sure. I'll let you know." Tori looked in the direction the waiter had gone. Eyeing the others around the table, she said, "Hey, you could have changed your wishes."

"I'm telling you," Nell said, reaching for a warm bread stick, "Tori emits pheromones."

"Forget about pheromones," Tori said, "we're celebrating Caroline's new lease, not my latest, um, encounter." She held up her water glass. "To surprises."

"Good ones," Nell said, raising her glass, too. "The kind that make you say 'Oh, my!' "

"Not 'Oh, dear,' " Pattie said, yawning.

"Or 'Oh, crap,' " Elaine grumbled.

"To surprises," Caroline repeated, looking once more at the ultrasound image of her baby.

It was the middle of July. She would be ready to see clients in another month, two at the most. She was enjoying the pace in

Harbor Woods. In fact, she liked the small-town atmosphere, and the way it had imploded with thousands of tourists and vacationers. There was little in the way of theater here, but Elaine and Tori assured her there were some fine off-off-Broadway plays in Traverse City. They insisted they would have to go soon, before Caroline entered her last trimester, and needed to visit the restroom every five minutes.

Caroline had never considered herself earthy, far from it, and yet just the other evening she'd happened to mention that the baby was kickboxing, and suddenly there were four pairs of hands on her abdomen. Every week she felt more a part of their circle.

She had satisfied nearly everything on her mental check list. She'd come to Harbor Woods and discovered Karl — although she was terribly worried about him. She'd made friends and had found a place to live. Soon, she would open her new law practice. Her life was unfolding. She never knew what the new day would bring, but more and more she felt certain she would be able to handle whatever came her way.

Caroline stopped on the pier to empty the sand from her Magli sandals. Bit by bit, the marina was waking up.

Waves washed onto the beach, flattening all that remained of a sand castle built the previous day. The early birds were up, as were the early-morning fishermen heading out to deep water. She'd encountered a few dog walkers on her way, and wondered if Shane would even be awake.

Her bag was packed, her gas tank full, her summerhouse locked up tight. There was one more thing she had to do before she left town.

She could see a light on through the port hole window. Since boats didn't have front doors, she knocked on the window.

He came out stretching and shrugging into a wrinkled T-shirt, his hair still wet. He took one look at her pale yellow pants and slightly clingy maternity top, and said, "Going someplace?"

"I have to go back to Chicago to take care of some things. I hate the thought of leaving Karl, but this has to be done, and soon."

"How long will you be gone?"

"Three or four days. Five at the most."

She looked past Shane where clouds gathered near the horizon. A storm was reportedly moving across the lake. If her grandfather were still alive, he would have been watching the storm from the double

French doors in his living room. She wondered what he'd thought about as he'd watched it rain. She imagined he'd been thinking about the past, and Anna, and Caroline's mother. Perhaps, once or twice, he'd been remembering climbing a water tower and writing something scandalous about a teacher he and his best friend hadn't liked.

"I'm ready to go," she said. "But I couldn't leave without telling you."

She could feel him watching her. The air was charged with something nearly as palpable as the approaching storm. "I'm worried about leaving Karl. I wouldn't go if I had a choice, but I have to make arrangements for the sale of my grandfather's house." She was rambling, and she made herself stop.

"I'll finish the book you're reading to Karl, Caroline. And I'll call you if there's any change."

Just like that, he put her mind at ease. She gave him a card containing her cell-phone number. "I'll see you when I get back."

"Have a safe trip home."

"Thanks. I'll try." These past few weeks Caroline had come to trust Shane. He was decent and honorable. Sometimes she wondered if Tori ever regretted divorcing him. It seemed to Caroline that regrets were part of life. The way growth and change were part of life. As she made her way to her car, she hoped she wouldn't encounter any surprises when she got to Chicago, or when she returned.

CHAPTER 12

Caroline stepped out of the way as the professional movers carried the last of the antique furniture out the front door. For two days, her grandfather's house in Lake Forest had been turned into an arena for a stately auction run by a well-known Chicago auction house. Everything had gone exactly as planned. In fact, the only surprise so far had been the amount some of the pieces brought.

The artwork Caroline hadn't wanted to keep had been consigned to a local gallery. The antiques that hadn't brought fair market value had been consigned to a reputable antiques dealer.

In the two months Caroline had been gone, she'd made inquiries and phone calls, and arranged for appraisals. She'd researched, interviewed and handled everything prior to today's final estate auction sale. Now, that was over, too.

She closed the front door, the heels of her Vera Wangs clicking over the parquet floor in the foyer, the sound echoing through the nearly empty house. Turning in a half circle, memories came to her from every direction. There she was at nine, bowing after her first piano recital. And there she was on the stairs before her high-school prom. And a few months later she'd stood at the front door, her cases loaded with everything she would need for her freshman year at Notre Dame. In the background in every memory stood Henry O'Shaughnessy, a quiet, steadfast, prideful presence. It was still impossible to fathom that he was gone.

The Aubusson rug, the Louis XIV dresser, her grandfather's favorite leather chair, and the other items she hadn't been able to part with were in storage. The house was empty without them, without him. The For Sale sign would go up first thing Monday morning. She was doing the right thing by selling the house.

Wouldn't Tori have loved to get her hands on a piece of property like this one? It was amazing how many times Caroline had thought of her friends these past three days. She'd spoken with Maria her first night in town. Lo and behold, her grandfather's former housekeeper was enrolled in summer semester at the local college. Life had a way of changing in the most surprising ways.

Upstairs, Caroline paused in the doorway of her grandfather's bedroom where a lamp, an old trunk and a stack of books, on top of which rested his reading glasses, were all that remained. With a hand resting on the rounding swell where her flat stomach used to be, she opened the attic door.

If she'd thought the downstairs echoed, it was nothing compared to the emptiness up here. The cleaning service had been very thorough. Even the dust that had floated on the air was gone. The only item left was the old desk in which she'd discovered that tin containing Anna's letter. It wasn't an antique, but Caroline hadn't been able to bear to let it go. She hadn't decided what to do with it.

There was no ventilation in the attic; the air was so hot it was difficult to breathe. Having no reason to linger, she retraced her steps down two flights of stairs. At the bottom, she didn't know where to turn.

She went to the French doors in the living room. Had it only been three months since she'd stood in exactly this spot, searching for a way to tell Steven about the baby?

Sometimes she wondered what would have happened if she'd gone first that day.

Fate had stepped in. Looking out at the sky still gray after the past two days' rain, Caroline had never been so relieved about anything in her life.

Fate was an amazing thing.

Besides, what good would have been served in telling Steven? She probably wouldn't have left Chicago. She wouldn't have discovered Karl. She wouldn't have shared morning tea or heard all his snippets of poignant memories. She wouldn't have met the girls, or leased space for her new law practice. She wouldn't have met Shane, either. She hadn't heard from him. In this case, no news was good news.

Now that she had the new perspective of time and distance, she found that Harbor Woods wasn't so different from Lake Forest. Lake Forest was by far larger, and its proximity to Chicago made it far more prime real estate. But the houses in both cities were old, stately and charming. And yet it seemed lifeless here.

Caroline realized it wasn't the city that was lifeless. It was that her life was no longer here.

The final movers were due to arrive in an hour. She didn't have any idea how to pass the time. There was no work in her briefcase, and literally no one to visit or call nearby.

How could she have lived in Chicago for thirty-five years and know no one? Well, no one special. She could have rattled off the names of a hundred people she knew here. And yet there wasn't one person she could call to while away an hour.

Her stomach rumbled. That was certainly no surprise. She seemed to be hungry a lot lately. The cupboards and refrigerator were empty. It was the middle of the day, too early for dinner and too late for lunch. A craving came out of nowhere.

Grabbing her purse and keys, she was off.

Delights Ice Cream Parlor hadn't changed in thirty-five years. Her grandfather used to bring her here after piano lessons and chess club. The parlor was old-fashioned, boasting glass-topped tables and wrought-iron chairs. It was Saturday, and it was crowded. Parents and their children claimed most of the tables, but one held a group of six women. Ordering a strawberry ice-cream cone, Caroline found herself studying them. They looked as different from each other as she, Nell, Elaine, Pattie and Tori probably looked to strangers. Their laughter, however, was the same.

Sitting by herself at a table near the back of the room, she licked her ice-cream cone and tried to decide what flavors the girls would be ordering if they were here. Pattie would order something healthy, like frozen yogurt. Elaine would probably want some pragmatic flavor like vanilla. Nell would have to have double-mocha fudge. It was hard to know what Tori would be in the mood for. One day she might want mint chocolate-chip and the next she'd munch on celery instead.

Suddenly a little boy and girl dressed alike dashed past her toward the open door. The frantic mother scooped up the little girl, but the boy slipped out of her reach. Without thinking, Caroline grabbed him up before he reached the door. He let out a screech as if this were a game, and Caroline found herself laughing, too.

She'd never done that before. Until recently, she'd rarely noticed children. "Twins?" she asked, handing the child back to his mother.

"Lord, yes. They're almost three. Thank you."

"They're both adorable." Caroline smiled into the most chocolaty faces she'd ever seen.

The commotion had drawn an audience.

She was about to return to her seat and slip out of her shoes when she noticed someone watching her across the room. Something about the shape of his head and the silver in his hair drew her attention a second time.

Steven.

Sourness settled to the pit of her stomach. Two young boys and a petite woman with short blond hair stood in front of him, busily ordering their ice cream.

Caroline could feel the color draining from her face, past the charm at her throat. It seemed to pool in the pit of her stomach. Before her discomfiture became obvious to everyone, she gave him a small smile, the kind she would have given any acquaintance, then returned to her seat.

As soon as she could do so without it appearing cowardly, she walked straight out the door.

There were roughly three million people living in greater Chicago. So of course it stood to reason she would run into the last person she wanted to see.

He wouldn't come here.

Caroline paced from one end of her grandfather's house to the other. Of course Steven wouldn't come here. Her dress had been loose fitting. He probably hadn't noticed what was underneath it. Besides, he'd been with Brenda and the boys. No, he wouldn't show up at her door.

What would she say to him if he did?

She drew a complete blank.

It didn't matter. He wouldn't come.

The movers were due to arrive at three. As soon as they finished, she would leave.

The doorbell chimed.

Rather than hurrying to open it, she looked at her watch. It was fifteen to. She took a deep breath and closed her eyes. Movers were notoriously late, not early. She knew before she opened the door who it would be.

Steven stood on the front stoop. He looked extremely polished and well dressed, urban, and he was also obviously shocked.

"Steven. This is a surprise."

"Is it?"

Of course it wasn't. That wasn't the point. No matter how much she'd reassured herself to the contrary, she'd known this moment would come the instant she saw him across that parlor. Steven Phillips wasn't one to let a sleeping dog lie. Cringing, she looked past him to his car.

"I'm alone. I dropped Brenda and the boys at the mall. May I come in?"

No, she thought. "Certainly," she said,

stepping back. "I would offer you a seat, but as you can see, the place is fairly empty."

"Standing is fine with me."

Meeting his eyes levelly, she said, "What brings you to Lake Forest?"

"Brenda and I are looking at houses in the area."

"You're moving out of the city?"

"Brenda has researched the suburbs. The school system here comes highly recommended."

"I can vouch for that. This house isn't on the market yet, however."

"I'm not interested in purchasing your grandfather's house, Caroline."

Silence.

Nerves churned in her stomach. It had been a long day. A long week. Her feet hurt. The pale yellow dress was one of her favorites, but there was a chocolate smudge on the short sleeve from a child's little hand. She probably looked a mess. She had a long drive ahead of her, and she wanted to go get out of Chicago before the traffic became unbearable.

"I was surprised to see you at the ice-cream parlor," he said. "I wasn't aware you'd returned to Chicago."

Oh, no he didn't. He wasn't intimidating her with that piercing stare.

"I only returned to put my grandfather's estate in order. Brenda and the boys looked well."

"I don't think she saw you."

Steven was a bull-dog in court. It was obvious who was in charge at home. Caroline couldn't believe she'd ever been remotely attracted to him.

She caught him looking at her bare ring finger, and then at her midsection. Finally, he looked her in the eye. "What's going on, Caroline?"

"What do you mean?"

"You take a leave of absence from the firm, leave Chicago on a whim, then resign from Hilliard, Ross and Whitley via long-distance. You've told no one you were going to have a child."

"I've told people, Steven."

"You didn't tell me."

She knew what was coming. Before he accused her of anything, she said, "So. Now you assume it's your child?"

"Is it?"

Neither of them had moved from the foyer, and their voices echoed in the nearly empty house. It occurred to her that this would be one of the last conversations she would have here. She wished it could have been a more pleasant one.

"Tell me, Steven, what would Brenda say about that?" He wasn't the only one who could be a bulldog.

"Let's leave Brenda out of this."

He was the one who mentioned her every few seconds. "You nearly missed me," she said. "The movers will be here any minute to take the last of my grandfather's things."

"I need to know, Caroline, for peace of mind, if nothing else."

Peace of mind. That rankled. "It isn't like you to jump to conclusions, Steven."

"That's right. It isn't. This is the worst possible time this could have happened. It isn't exactly the sort of thing conducive to saving my marriage. If it's mine, you should have told me in the beginning. We could have discussed your options when we had still had options. What am I supposed to tell Brenda? What about the boys?"

Caroline harbored no illusions about Steven, about his feelings for her or her baby, but if he didn't stop being so damn considerate of Brenda and his boys, she was going to have to wrap her fingers around his skinny neck and choke him. "Don't tell them anything."

"Do you want me to pretend I didn't see you?"

"Of course not."

"Then you expect me to turn around and walk away with *don't tell them anything?*" he asked, his tone growing more severe.

"Yes, I do."

"Then it isn't mine?"

For a moment, she hated him for sounding so damn hopeful.

"Can you look me in the eye and say it, Caroline?"

Struggling with her uncertainty, Caroline looked him in the eye. A sense of calm came over her, and she heard herself utter the last thing she'd expected to say.

CHAPTER 13

"You really looked him in the eye and said that?"

"Yes, word for word," Caroline said.

While Caroline and Elaine spoke, church bells sounded in the distance.

"You told him it isn't his child?"

"Yes. I told him it isn't his child." Caroline hadn't intended to bring up the incident. In fact, she hadn't planned to see the girls today. As expected, the movers had been late. By the time she left Chicago, everyone else seemed to be trying to leave, too. She hadn't gotten back to Harbor Woods until the wee hours of the morning. After sleeping for a few hours, she'd showered and dressed and come here to try to decide how to best use the space.

The details regarding how Elaine, Tori, Nell and Pattie had found her were still slightly sketchy, but when Caroline had heard the old-fashioned bell jangle over the door of her new office and discovered them standing on the other side of it, she decided to give them a quick tour, then bow out to visit Karl. Somewhere between the reception area and the offices she would use as her private suite, the entire sordid tale came tumbling out. Caroline couldn't blame any of them for looking skeptical.

"You lied?" Nell asked.

"I told him what he wanted to hear," Caroline said. "He knows it was a bold-faced lie."

"He does?" This time it was Tori who couldn't seem to close her gaping mouth.

Caroline sat on the edge of Karl's old desk. Resting her palms on the smooth surface on either side of her legs, she said, "Steven has an uncanny ability to sniff out the smallest loophole, untruth, white lie or fabrication. It's one of the qualities that makes him so good at what he does. It's a reputation he relishes, and he's earned it, along with a great deal of money for his clients, which in turn, has made him a very wealthy man, and one of the most sought after litigation consultants in Chicago."

"So he knew you were lying," Tori said.

"Yes."

"You're sure."

"Absolutely," Caroline said quite simply.

"How can you know for sure?" Elaine asked, curious now.

"I've seen him in action in court and out of it. He knows. And he knows I know he knows."

"This is scaring me," Tori said. "Because that made sense to me."

"And he just walked away, relieved of all monetary obligation and moral responsibility," Nell whispered.

Caroline nodded again.

"Good riddance," Elaine insisted, the expression on her narrow face earnest and sincere.

The other three all murmured some form of agreement. Caroline wasn't accustomed to such loyalty, but she was learning to accept it, and appreciate it.

During the long drive from Chicago, she'd thought about that confrontation with Steven. She *had* told him what he'd wanted to hear, and in doing so, in a sense it became true. This child was hers, and hers alone. Her baby hadn't been conceived to break up a family, but to make one. A family of two.

"In a way, you're lucky," Elaine said. "If you never marry, you'll never have to worry about getting a divorce. Divorce is hell."

Nell and Tori seconded that.

"When will you be ready to see clients?" Elaine asked.

Caroline looked around the old suite of offices. The place was dull and dusty. The tin ceilings were original, the moldings and window casings wide. Each office was fitted with a door that contained etched glass intended to guard clients' privacy. Caroline could easily picture Karl seeing clients here, but she planned to make a few updates in order to bring it into the current century.

"I'll hang my shingle as soon as I receive the paperwork from the Michigan State Bar Association. I expect to hear within the month. Why?"

"I confronted Justin."

"Oh, Elaine," Nell said.

"How?" Tori asked.

"When?" Pattie said.

"And you waited until now to tell us?" Nell implored.

"It happened just last night. He denied it, until I showed him my little Polaroids."

"Oh, honey," Nell sympathized, her eyes pools of appeal in her pretty round face. "What did he say?"

"He doesn't want a divorce."

"He doesn't?" Pattie said.

"He assured me she isn't someone he would ever leave me for. It seems she isn't marriage material. As if that was some big compliment to me. Apparently he wants us both."

"Of course he does," Tori said derisively. "A dutiful wife and a piece on the side. What slimeball wouldn't want that?"

"Elaine?" This time it was Caroline who spoke. "The question is, what do you want?"

"She can have him," Elaine said quietly. "All of him. I want you to find a loophole in that prenup. I want him to know how it feels to get royally screwed."

"Atta girl," Pattie cut in.

"Drop that agreement off at my summerhouse," Caroline said. "I can start working on it before I'm officially open for business."

Caroline's cell phone rang. After fishing the small device out of her purse, she placed it to her ear. She recognized Shane's voice.

"Are you back?"

"I got in late last night."

"It's about Karl, Caroline."

Foreboding crept over her. For one blinding instant, she wished she hadn't taken the call. "Is he —"

"Yes," he said. "He's gone."

"When?" she whispered.

"I just received the call. When he didn't come to breakfast, they went looking for him. Evidently he died in his sleep."

"Where are you?" she asked Shane.

"On my boat."

"I'll be right there."

Hanging up, desolation swept over her. She'd known this was coming. And yet she wasn't prepared. The doctor had given Karl another two months. It had only been two weeks. It was too soon. There was so much Karl hadn't told her, so much she couldn't tell him.

A hot tear rolled down her cheek. "I have to go."

"What's wrong?"

"He died."

"Who, honey?" Nell asked gently.

"My grandfather."

She picked up her purse by rote, and somehow managed to follow her friends out the door. After locking up, she started for her car.

Behind her, she heard Elaine say, "I thought her grandfather died months ago."

Caroline was too far away to hear the rest. Pointing her car toward the marina, she felt an unsettling sense of déjà vu.

Half the county turned out for Karl's funeral service. Cars were lined up on both sides of the lane, stretching all the way from the No Trespassing sign at the gate of the lighthouse property to the county road.

The private gravel lane had been scraped, the dust laid by a rain shower overnight. Karl Peterson had requested to be cremated, and he'd wanted a quiet service, and as little fuss as possible, but R. J. Clark was the county commissioner, and he and Karl went way back, and while R.J. couldn't take credit for the rain, by God, he'd said, scraping the lane was the least the county could do.

Karl's wasn't a typical funeral. There had been no three-day mourning period for the cantankerous old attorney. "When the time comes, get it over with," he'd told Shane the year he'd turned eighty.

So, the day after Shane had called to tell Caroline the sad news, she found herself sitting with hundreds of other people in makeshift rows of folding chairs that had been set up on the lawn near the lighthouse. There had been no formal viewing, although she and Shane had gone to his room at the manor one last time to say goodbye before he'd been taken to be cremated. The money most people spent on a casket and all the trimmings had been donated discreetly to a safe house for battered women. Of course, it was brought up at the service this afternoon.

Caroline had expected Shane to give the eulogy. After all, it was Shane whom Karl had trusted with his final wishes, and with his care in his final months. But Shane didn't speak, and she realized he preferred it that way.

She saw him in the distance. He stood to one side near the front with three men she didn't recognize. He wore a dark suit, white shirt and a tie. If she wasn't mistaken, he was wearing socks. She couldn't bring herself to smile. She couldn't bring herself to cry, either. She remembered how long it had taken her to finally break down after her grandfather's funeral three months ago.

Karl Peterson's funeral was as different from Henry O'Shaughnessy's as it could be. One had been held in a church and had been attended by judges and businessmen and some of the wealthiest people in Chicago, the other on the grounds of the beloved lighthouse where two young men had once dreamed. Karl had wanted a simple ending. Caroline was of the opinion that there was no easy way to say goodbye.

It was almost too beautiful a day for such a sad event. Waves lapped the shore lazily, and sailboats with bright orange sails glided in and out of view. There were no flowers. Again, charitable donations were accepted and encouraged instead. Although he'd made Karl's wishes clear regarding a simple service, Shane had been outvoted. It seemed people needed to give Karl a good send-off.

As Caroline listened to the stories they told about the man who had been such an integral part of Harbor Woods for so long, she didn't see how Karl could mind. He'd been well liked and highly respected, although at times he had been a thorn in some people's sides. Many of the people gathered here this afternoon would probably honestly miss him. She wondered where they'd all been these past nine months while he'd been living at Woodland Country Manor. As far as she knew, few of them had visited Karl then. But such was the way of people.

Other than Shane and the two nurses who'd cared for Karl, the only person Caroline recognized was Tori. She hadn't seen her until the sheriff finished saying a few words. Tori's hair looked gorgeous against her black sheath. Caroline almost smiled to herself, because only Tori Young could look so stunning at a funeral.

By now Caroline wasn't surprised to see her friend squeeze in next to Shane. She said something to him, and he tilted his head, positioning his ear close to her mouth in order to hear. Caroline didn't believe for a minute that Tori hated her former husband. Whatever was wrong between them stemmed from something other than hatred.

As far as Caroline could tell, Nell, Elaine and Pattie weren't there. But of course they wouldn't be. They lived and worked in Charlevoix, and they didn't know that Karl Peterson had been Caroline's grandfather. Although she'd spoken to them briefly last night, she'd decided not to share that information, saying simply that her loss was on her mother's side and that Caroline hadn't known him well.

She half expected Tori to put it together. Actually, she wished she would.

There had been a lovely write-up in this morning's newspaper. The headline had read Saying Goodbye To One Of Our Own. The article took up most of the front page.

Shane had asked Caroline if she wanted to be listed in the obituary. After thinking about it, she'd told him no, for her relationship to Karl wasn't common knowledge. It didn't sadden her that nobody else knew. It saddened her that Karl hadn't.

She sighed. She'd been doing that a lot these past few days.

The service ended, and everyone stood. The sheriff was shaking Shane's hand.

Caroline didn't see Tori anywhere.

While many of the mourners congregated into small groups, Caroline slipped away, alone.

Caroline didn't go to Tori's for girl's night on Thursday evening. Evidently Tori was feuding with Andy and Shane, and Pattie's daughter had swimmer's ear, whatever that was. Nell and Elaine had decided to see a movie. They'd kindly invited Caroline along. She'd declined.

When she heard the knock on her door at half-past nine, she half expected it to be them. She couldn't see whoever was on her front stoop from her kitchen window, but she could see the driveway, and she knew of only one person in Harbor Woods who drove an old silver Shelby Mustang.

"Hi," she said, opening the door to Shane.

"Hi."

It had been nearly a week since Karl died. She'd stopped by the marina a few days ago to say hello. Shane's phone had barely stopped ringing long enough to return her greeting. Now that there was no reason to go to the nursing home, they didn't run into each other. Perhaps she could have taken up the search for Anna's diary, but it seemed like a moot point now. Anna was gone. Henry was gone. And Karl was gone. What difference would the diary make now?

"Would you like to come in?" she asked.

"I can't."

"Is something wrong?"

A look of discomfort crossed his face. "I just had a hell of a fight with Vickie. After that, I got into it with Andy. Some of the people who rent slips got together and filed a complaint against another boat owner. I had to talk to the guy. Let's just say he wasn't happy. Three reamings in one day is a lot to take, even for me."

Standing in the doorway on a quiet summer night, listening to Shane complain, she was struck by how good it was to see him. "You've had a bad day," she said. "You stopped by, but you don't want to come in."

"I thought I'd take my boat out. It seems only fitting that you should come."

"Fitting, how?"

"He was your grandfather, Caroline."

Understanding dawned. Karl's final request was to have his ashes scattered across the night waters of Lake Michigan. Shane was about to honor that request. It was all Caroline could do to squeeze one word past the lump in her throat. "When?"

"What are you doing right now? Karl loved summer nights. The sky is clear. And the moon will be up by the time we get out there."

"Do I need to bring anything?"

"I have everything we'll need, Caroline."

"If it gets too cool for you," Shane said when they were a few hundred yards from shore, "I can close up the cabin."

"No," Caroline said, peering through the open windows. "I like it."

It was fifteen degrees cooler on Lake Michigan than on land, and the breeze felt good on her face. She wore a life jacket, navy slacks and canvas shoes that were comfortable and perfect for boating. The wind was fast undoing her hair, which she'd fastened in a clip at her nape.

Shane operated the cruiser with the finesse of someone who knew his way around boats and the water. He wore his regular attire of faded blue jeans and sandals. They hadn't spoken about what he planned to do, but she'd seen him place an urn in a compartment for safekeeping. She remembered all the publicity the Kennedys had received when they'd wanted to spread the ashes of their loved ones over the ocean off the Cape. They'd been granted special permission. Of course, they were the Kennedys.

"You realize," she said, "that what you're

proposing is technically illegal."

Next to her, Shane said, "Karl knew the rules. He was eighty-five. He lived a long, clean life, and died of old age, not some horrific contagious disease." He raised his voice in order to be heard over the engine and the wind. "Ashes to ashes, dust to dust. I gave him my word. Don't think of it as breaking the law. Think of it as bending it."

"First I lied to Steven," she said, "and now I'm about to *bend* the law."

They didn't speak again for a long time. Caroline didn't know how Shane kept his bearings, but he checked gauges and instruments, adjusting his course accordingly. After some time had passed, he began to slow down. A few minutes later, he cut the engine. "We're here."

Caroline peered in every direction. There was only water, sky and darkness. She had no idea where "here" was. "Karl chose this exact place?"

"If it was daylight, and we had binoculars, and you looked straight that way," he said, pointing, "you would be able to see Karl's lighthouse."

Shane took the urn from the compartment. And then he reached for her hand, holding it tightly as they stepped up, out of the cabin.

On deck, he guided her hand to the railing. "Is it okay if I let go?"

She nodded. "As long as I can hold on to something. I don't have my sea legs."

"Relax your knees. Ride the rocking motion. Don't fight it."

"That's easier said than done." But she tried.

"Ready?" he asked as he opened the urn.

No, she wasn't. How could anyone be truly ready to do something so final? But she nodded.

"Would you like to say something, Caroline?"

She pictured a red-haired boy taking a trip for supplies with his father, and a red-haired man falling in love with a girl who had no idea she would soon be facing a heartbreaking decision. She pictured him climbing the water tower with his best friend, and later, representing people who couldn't pay him. She imagined him opening that letter from home. She remembered him sipping Earl Grey, and falling asleep in the middle of something he was telling her.

She shook her head, for she had nothing to say that would do him justice.

Shane flung the contents of the urn into the air, scattering the ashes into the darkness, where they fell to the moonlit water before sinking out of sight. "Goodbye, old man," he said. "Thanks for everything. I'm going to miss you."

Emotion welling in her chest, Caroline looked, not at the water, but at the moon. She already missed him. "I'm glad I knew you, Grandfather."

She and Shane remained exactly as they were, waves rocking the boat, the night infinitely dark and still. She couldn't help thinking how vast the universe was, and how small humans were. It occurred to her that it had always been this way. Society changed, but life and death remained the same.

Feeling Shane looking at her, she waited for him to say something profound.

"Caroline?"

"Yes?"

"Who's Steven?"

She glanced at him, surprised. For some reason, she started to laugh. "He's nobody."

"Nobody."

She nodded even as she began to tell him about Steven's visit in Lake Forest. She wound up telling Shane about her grandfather's funeral three months ago, and Steven's little bombshell later that day. She told Shane about resigning from Hilliard, Ross and Whitley, and how it had felt to discover that Karl was alive. She talked and talked, the wind in her hair, the moon on the water, her voice quieting to little more than a whisper as she said, "If he'd cared, I might feel differently, but he didn't. Steven's nobody to me. Not anymore."

"In that case, there's no sense standing around talking about nobody."

He took her hand again, and led her safely inside. She stood out of his way as he closed the windows and prepared for the return trip.

"Caroline?" he said again.

She turned around. And honestly, she never saw his kiss coming.

CHAPTER 14

Shane and Caroline had been quiet during the drive to her house. It was after midnight, and she hadn't left the light on over the summerhouse door. The moon lit their way, casting their shadows in intricate detail on the ground, their shoes crunching on crushed shells along the path. He reached for her hand, holding just her fingers in his loose grasp. Caroline closed her eyes at the tenderness the gesture brought to the backs of her eyes and the base of her throat.

It had been an emotional night, and yet releasing Karl's ashes over the lake he'd loved had felt right. As unexpected as Shane's kiss had been, it had felt right, too. That was what worried her, for he'd kissed her as if the touch of his lips on hers was integral to his nature, to the moment, to who he was and what she was to him.

"You aren't going to invite me in, are you?" he asked.

There was no sense wondering how he'd known. She'd given that a great deal of thought during the quiet drive. She'd assumed pregnant women felt maternal. In fact, she could attest to an indescribable depth of maternal love for her child. This desire was a different matter. It was absurd, and yet she felt that if she did ask him in, she would somehow be cheating Tori. "No, Shane, I'm not."

He heaved the kind of sigh only men could manage.

"If it's any consolation," she said, recalling how much easier it had been to keep her balance during the boat ride back to the marina. "I think I may have discovered the secret to gaining my sea legs, and I have you to thank for it."

Assuming a stance she recognized, feet planted comfortably, hands on his hips, shoulders back slightly, he said, "Now that's a new term for it."

"Good night, Shane."

"It didn't start out that way, but it's ending well, all things considered. Good night, Caroline."

She let herself in. After she prepared for bed, she tried Tori's cell number. When it went straight to her voice mail, Caroline hung up, for this wasn't exactly something she could say in a message. One of these days soon, she needed to talk to her in person.

"Welcome mothers, fathers, sisters, friends, significant others." The nurse in charge of the expectant parenting class cast a pointed look in Caroline's direction.

"We're just friends," Tori called.

Caroline was never one-hundred-percent certain what Tori might do or say. A scamp one minute, a fiercely loyal champion of the underdog the next, she'd agreed to attend the prenatal classes and act as Caroline's birthing coach.

The six-week course would cover everything from the third trimester to the postnatal checkup. There was a lot to learn about giving birth, and much of it wasn't pretty. Tori assured her that experiencing it personally wasn't as bad as watching it on video. That was good to know, since the woman on the television screen was screaming.

"Then she's acting?" Caroline whispered.

"I doubt it. Can you say epidural? Forget natural childbirth. If they offer you drugs, take them."

The couple next to them shushed them. Somehow, Caroline didn't think she and Tori were going to be teacher's pets.

During the break, the mothers and their labor coaches were supposed to practice their relaxation breathing techniques. Looking around the room at all the women lying on their backs, Tori said, "Man, this almost makes me want another baby."

"Seriously?" Caroline asked, breathing in, breathing out.

"Seriously."

"Do you have a father in mind?"

Tori shrugged. "I was seeing someone, but the spark's gone."

"Already?"

"Like always, it fizzled fast," Tori said.

While everyone was getting situated in sitting positions on their mats, Caroline said, "Would you ever consider trying again with Andy's father?"

"Trying what? You mean a reconciliation?"

"Yes," Caroline said. "Perhaps what you feel for him isn't hatred."

"Of course it isn't hatred."

Caroline held her breath as she waited for the opportunity to casually mention that she knew Shane.

"But it sure as hell isn't love, either. What's all this talk about relationships?" Tori asked. "Are you falling in love with somebody?"

Love? Caroline wanted to scream, because

now there was no way to broach the subject subtly. It had been a week since she and Shane had scattered Karl's ashes. Caroline would have liked Tori's blessing. She got the distinct impression that would be a very cold day in hell.

"Are you?" Tori asked.

"*Love* is a strong word."

"Are you thinking about having sex?"

If Caroline had been drinking a soda, she would have sprayed the people in front of her.

"Women have needs, too," Tori whispered. "Surely you've discovered another use for the handheld shower nozzle. Are you blushing? Good grief, are you innocent or what?"

Caroline didn't feel innocent, exactly. She felt on the brink of discovery. It seemed as though she'd found a kindred spirit in Shane, if such spirits existed. Perhaps it was as he'd said on the lake last week. Maybe she'd simply discovered a partner in crime. Then again, perhaps Tori was right, and she was falling in love.

Caroline hyperventilated. A dozen people crowded around her to help her breathe through it. Practicing the newly learned technique, she couldn't help wondering if there had ever been a cold day in hell.

■ ■ ■ ■

Shane opened the window in Karl's old bedroom. It was hotter than blazes in here. It had been more than a week since he and Caroline had scattered Karl's ashes, and she was helping him sort through Karl's things. Shane was boxing up the clothes and she was working on the books in the living room. He recognized the tactic for what it was. She was keeping a respectable distance between them.

Darkness had fallen a while ago. Cicadas and crickets chirruped from their hiding places outdoors. It was amazing how much racket a lone moth could make banging its head against the screen as it tried to get to the light inside. Nobody understood the insect's futility better than Shane.

He emptied the last dresser drawer. Hoisting the cardboard box into his arms, he carried it to the dining room and stacked it with the others. Taking a breather, he stretched, rotating a kink or two from the back of his neck. It may have been a ploy, but it was an effective one, for it gave him a reason to linger where Caroline was in plain view.

She hadn't made a lot of progress with

the packing. Instead of filling a box with books, she'd opened a volume and was reading. She was like that, so thirsty and open to literature and history and folklore, anything old or new.

She turned slightly, presenting him with a side view. She was more than five-and-a-half months along now. She hadn't gained a great deal of weight, but she was still obviously a pregnant woman. A beautiful pregnant woman. Her shirt was red, the front dipping to a V that crisscrossed between her breasts and snugged her body below them. Who the hell's idea it was to make maternity clothes sexy, he didn't know, but he wouldn't have minded doing a little exploring. Either there was something seriously wrong with him or there was something seriously right about his feelings for her. He didn't know which possibility bothered him more.

Needing to think about something else, he had a sudden mental picture of Vickie, a mood buster if there ever was one. "I tried to talk to Andy about college the other day. It went about as well as when I tried to talk about it with his mother."

Caroline looked over at him but didn't close the book.

"She's on a new kick," he said. "Now she

wants him to go out for football."

"Is she hoping he'll earn a scholarship?" Caroline asked, obviously not following.

"That's what she says. But that's not the real reason." Shane entered the living room. "Vic's upset because Andy doesn't hang out with his friends. She's afraid that means there's something deeply and profoundly wrong with him. She wants him to make new friends, and she thinks joining a team is the answer. Football practice is starting in a few weeks."

"Does Andy enjoy football?"

A table lamp was on in the corner, as well as the floor lamp across the room. Neither quite dispensed with the shadows between them. "At first he rode my butt into the ground on our bikes, and I'm pretty sure he enjoyed doing it. But I don't think he has the killer instinct for football. Which is what I told Vickie. She told me I never back her up, and then she hung up on me."

"Shane, I —"

"I don't usually bad-mouth Andy's mother. I suppose she can't help it that she's a pain in the ass."

Caroline closed the book she'd been reading and placed it in the cardboard carton. When Shane reached his hand toward her, she froze. His touch was light, his fingertips barely grazing her skin just below her neck. He took the charm dangling from the end of its delicate chain between his thumb and forefinger.

The next thing she knew, his mouth came down hard on hers. She felt herself being propelled backward until her back touched the wall. His legs straddled hers, pinning her there while his arms cushioned her, protecting her.

His face was so close to hers she could see her own reflection in his eyes. She stiffened, and he said, "Am I hurting you?"

He meant because of the baby.

She shook her head.

"Something tells me you're going to give me the 'don't' speech again."

She didn't know whether to roll her eyes or swat him. "Tori is a friend of mine."

"Who?" He settled more intimately against her.

"Tori. Your ex-wife?"

At least she finally had his attention. "What does Vickie have to do with this?"

"I know her as Tori. She was the first person to befriend me in Harbor Woods. Until recently, I didn't know she was your ex-wife."

"Do you want my condolences?"

Now she did swat him.

"I noticed you said ex-wife," he said. "*Ex* being the key word. I don't see a problem."

Of course he didn't.

In an effort to move out of his embrace, she bumped the framed artwork behind her with so much force it swung like a pendulum on the nail. In a reflex action, Shane held the print in place with his left hand.

Behind the print was a door, slightly ajar. Opening it, he said, "I believe we just discovered Karl's secret hiding place."

She moved out of the way, and he lifted the print off its nail. An old wall safe with a broken lock was now in plain view. Inside was a leather diary and yellowed newspaper clippings. Removing the stack carefully, Caroline looked through them.

She was featured in every one.

"He knew," she said, scanning them one at a time. "He must have known my mother was his child." She looked at Shane. "Karl knew who I was."

She carried the tear sheets to the table, spreading them out evenly. Her entire life, beginning with her birth announcement and ending with a high-profile case she'd won last year had been clipped and saved in chronological order. The final press release must have come just before he'd suffered his stroke.

The evidence was straightforward and conclusive. Karl had known she was his granddaughter. There was no other explanation. She doubted he'd recognized her these past months, when his memories had been interrupted due to his stroke, but the man who'd amassed these clippings had known.

She looked at the wall safe again. Some people became eccentric with age. She'd once read of a small fortune the unsuspecting heirs of a miserly old woman had discovered when cleaning out her house following her death. She'd hidden money everywhere. They'd found seventy-five-thousand dollars in small bills, in her books, in her pillow cases, even in her shoes. Karl hadn't amassed cash. His collection was more precious than money.

"He not only knew you were his granddaughter," Shane said, quietly scanning the array spread out before him. "He was proud of you, too."

She thought about the way people were always trying to rush situations. Karl and Henry had had infinite patience. Neither had felt the need to tell her outright, and yet in their own good time, they'd sent her on a treasure hunt. It began with that first letter Henry had stored in an old tin in the attic in Lake Forest. It was as if he'd known it would lead her to Harbor Woods and all the rest. Caroline doubted the men had been in contact, and yet they couldn't have devised a better strategy if they'd written their plan on the water tower in green paint.

The clues had brought her a treasure trove that was her family history. Anna had died young, but first she'd left behind a legacy. That legacy had been Caroline's mother, Elsa, the seed planted by Karl, to be raised by Henry. Elsa had died young, also, but first she'd had a daughter, too. And so it went, Caroline's delicate lifeline and family tree. Now she was going to have a child. She'd never been more certain she was in the place she was meant to be, doing what she was meant to do.

She gestured to the table. "All of this happened because a boy and a girl happened to fall in love. A horrible war happened to separate them. And when she discovered she was pregnant, she married her child's best friend. It doesn't feel like happenstance. It feels like the unfolding of a master plan. And here I am."

"Here you are."

He was looking at her mouth, and it brought her full circle. But where exactly did this leave them?

She gathered up the articles and press

releases as gently as she'd spread them out. Placing the diary on top, she heard Shane closing the windows in the next room. She waited for him at the door. He locked it behind them, then took her elbow as if to insure she didn't stumble down the cement steps. He wasn't a man who wasted words. She could tell by his expression that they hadn't finished their discussion about Tori.

By the time they drove from Prospect Street to the Oval Lake Channel, she was ready to try to make him understand.

"Shane, what you and I have —"

"What you and I have has nothing to do with Vickie. You said it yourself a little while ago."

She should have known he wouldn't let her finish.

"It doesn't feel like happenstance." He quoted her, word for word. "It feels like the unfolding of a master plan."

"I was referring to Henry and Anna and Karl."

"It reaches all the way to us, Caroline, and you know it. I'm not surprised Vickie befriended you. She's like that. I fell for her hard myself. We were married for eleven years. She ended it because she just plain didn't love me, and never had."

"I think it goes deeper than that, Shane. I

244

think there's something in herself she doesn't love."

They were standing at her door, her key in her hand.

"You're the first woman I've wanted to be with since Vickie."

The declaration stunned her, but only for a moment. "In four years?" she asked.

"I wasn't kidding about monkdom."

Heaven help her, but she smiled.

"I don't take sex lightly, Caroline. If you invite me in, it's because it means something."

What he meant was that if she invited him in, it would be because *he* meant something. To her. And vice versa.

Despite her legal background and her courtroom training, her communication skills deserted her. She had the presence of mind to unlock the door, though. Evidently, it was all the invitation he needed.

He didn't kiss her until they reached her bedroom, and then only for a moment. She dispensed with the buttons on his shirt as quickly as he dispensed with hers. He took over from there — his shoes and jeans went next. He barely waited for her to shimmy out of her slacks and kick off her sandals before lowering her to the bed.

Caroline could count on one hand the

men she'd been with. In her experience, the first time was always slightly awkward. Her experience hadn't prepared her for Shane, whose pleasure was pure, his enjoyment a crescendo of the senses, of touch and sound and instinct. Their lovemaking was unrehearsed, uninhibited, undeniably unrestrained. At the heart of it all, he was careful, mindful of her condition.

Afterward, he rested his cheek on her belly. It was an act of reverence, of tenderness, and it touched her even more than the sex had.

The baby rolled beneath his cheek. Shane lifted his head. "He just kicked me."

Their gazes met. "I'll bet it's been a while since you've felt that, huh?" she asked.

He nodded. "You're worried about what Vickie will say about this, aren't you? Don't be. I'll tell her."

Her fingers splayed through his hair. "I should be the one to tell her, Shane."

There was no turning back now.

A week later, Caroline was opening the first carton of Karl's books. Shane placed the last box on the floor in her new suite of offices, pausing to say, "Have you seen Tori, yet?"

She shook her head. "An entire week, and

I haven't had a moment alone with her. Every time I call her she's either going to a closing or getting ready to show a house."

She picked up a certificate in a black frame. Looking at the four walls, she carried it to a waiting nail. She'd just received notification that she'd successfully waived into the Michigan State Bar Association. She would be ready to see clients soon. "What's a law practice without books?" Shane had asked when he'd shown up with Karl's collection.

"What a gift, Shane. Thank you."

She was the gift.

He and Vickie had just had a hell of a row at the marina. After she left, he'd thrown every wrench he owned. He wouldn't have let it get to him if it were just a matter of her pushing his buttons. This was about Andy. He and Vickie never saw eye-to-eye when it came to their son. Shane had needed to go for a spin on the lake or better yet, take a dive off the cliffs. He'd had to settle for a drive in his Shelby. He'd headed for the open road. Somehow he'd ended up at Caroline's office downtown.

She wore a simple summer dress and shoes he hadn't seen before. The woman must own a hundred different pairs of shoes. He used to tell himself he'd never get tangled up with a high-maintenance woman again. It wasn't high or low maintenance that made him keep coming back to Caroline. He'd spent five minutes in her presence this evening, and already he could feel the tension draining out of him. It was the same whenever he saw her. Every time her eyes rested on him, he felt the pull, the draw, the age-old lure of a man to a woman. He wanted her. It was that simple.

He hadn't had this much sex since — he couldn't remember if he'd ever had this much sex. He might have chalked it up to making up for lost time, except he didn't want just sex. He wanted Caroline. While he was at it, he wanted to ease the worry lines in her forehead.

"What are you doing tonight?" he asked.

"I have a parenting class. Afterward, I'm going to talk to Tori if I have to tie her to a chair. Now go on," she said. But she smiled. "Get out of here. I'd just as soon she didn't see us together until after I've talked to her."

"We're not doing anything wrong, Caroline."

Caroline told herself the same thing fifty times a day. Legally, it was the truth. Morally, and ethically, too. But it wasn't really about Caroline and Shane. Most people believed Tori was hard as nails. She wasn't.

There was a place inside her that wasn't hard at all.

"All right," he said, finally getting the message. "Go ahead and tell her. I'll stop over later."

"You'd better let me call you. This could take a while." Caroline had been rehearsing her speech for days. And she still wasn't sure what she would say. Whatever she said, she would do it as soon as her birthing class was over.

CHAPTER 15

Tori's mind had been miles away all evening. Caroline wasn't the only one who'd noticed. Several of the expectant mothers and a few of the fathers had asked if she was all right.

"What's going on?" Caroline whispered during break.

"It's Andy."

"Do you need to leave?"

Tori shook her head.

Tonight's class dealt with delivery by cesarean section and other high-risk birth situations. Those scenarios scared Caroline. This was her one chance at motherhood. Unlike some of the other mothers who complained about swollen ankles and stretch marks and just wanted the whole process to be over with, Caroline was enjoying being pregnant. She ate right, exercised and rested. Last night she and Shane had spent an hour lying on her bed, watching

250

her belly shift as her baby stretched and rolled and kicked from within.

Caroline had seen the midwife again this morning. Alice Cavanaugh had drawn more blood, as a precautionary measure, she'd assured Caroline. "Everything's going according to schedule," the other woman had said.

Caroline paid close attention to this evening's lecture. Tori didn't pay attention at all. Caroline wondered if she suspected, then told herself that was absurd. If Tori *had* suspected, she would have been sarcastic, perhaps even snide, but she wouldn't have been quiet.

They had tentative plans to go to the movies with Nell, Elaine and their girls after class. Caroline doubted that would happen once Tori had been told. "What time does the movie start?" she asked.

"Eight-fifteen."

That left them half an hour to talk. "Let's go someplace to talk. Are you familiar with the park at the mouth of Oval Lake channel?"

"Are you kidding? Houses around it are prime real estate."

Caroline wondered if it would be better to blurt it out right here. But Tori was already leaving the building, heading for her car.

Riding along, Caroline looked at Tori's profile. Normally, Victoria Young was the one offering advice or making pointed comments designed to draw a smirk or a smile. She was doing neither tonight.

Since discovering those newspaper clipping two weeks ago, a change had come over Caroline. Certainly part of it had to do with the knowledge that Karl had known he'd had a daughter, and eventually a granddaughter. He'd known love, honest work, friendship and contentment in his life. For the first time in her life, Caroline knew the feeling. In less than three months, her baby would arrive. It was hard to believe how much her life had changed since her child's conception.

She took a seat in an Adirondack chair beneath an old hickory tree. After Tori sat, too, Caroline looked up into the canopy. "Before I moved here, I wouldn't have known this was a hickory tree. One day I struck up a conversation with an old man who always throws his dog a stick. He told me his father planted this very tree when he was a young boy. You'll recognize the old man if he comes by, because he always wears black socks with his Nikes."

Tori stared straight ahead. "No one ever really knows what it's like to walk in someone else's shoes."

Caroline didn't know where that had come from, but it was the perfect opening. "I want to talk to you about that."

"I blew it," Tori said as if she hadn't heard.

"You. What?"

"Did I ever tell you I only gained nineteen pounds during my pregnancy?" Tori asked.

"I think you did, but Tori, I —"

"I wore my regular jeans home from the hospital. Not that my body will ever be the same. I was in labor for thirty-two hours. The epidural didn't work. I thought I was going to die."

Treading lightly, Caroline said, "Was it worth it, Tori?"

Tori got a look in her eyes Caroline had never seen. "It was the best thing I've ever done. There's no one on earth as strong as a woman giving birth. You know what you have to do and you do it." Her voice changed slightly, deepening as if she might cry. "I'd give anything to be that strong, that sure where Andy's concerned again."

Caroline was getting a really bad feeling. "What's happened? What's wrong?"

"When Andy was small, Shane and I used to take him over to the lighthouse. There's this huge outcropping of rocks there. Andy and his best friend used to pretend it was a giant turned to stone by its enemies. They made magic potions out of crushed shells and weeds and lake water. Shane would get us close in the boat, and the boys would fling the concoction at the rocks. By then, they believed it contained the secret ingredient that would awaken the sleeping beast. Now Andy looks at me as if I'm the monster."

Caroline still didn't understand whatever was at the root of the problems between Tori and Andy.

"He used to love me. He used to adore me. Even after the divorce, we got along so well. This afternoon he told me he hates me."

Caroline closed her eyes for a moment. "People say things in anger they don't mean."

"He meant it. He's hated me for a while. Two years to be exact."

"I can't imagine anyone hating you." She doubted Tori heard.

"Shane believes time heals. How does time heal blame?"

"Blame?" Caroline asked.

Tori stared straight ahead. "It was windy that day. I shouldn't have let the boys go sailing. They'd taken boating safety courses, and they'd sailed dozens of times. That day

I had a bad feeling. I shouldn't have let them go."

Part of Caroline didn't want to ask. "What happened that day?"

"There was an accident. Brian went overboard."

"It wasn't your fault. It couldn't have been." Caroline's voice was barely more than a whisper.

"Did I ever tell you Andy's best friend's name was Brian Kerrigan? He and Andy were inseparable. They were best friends, but they were closer than brothers. They did everything together, and that day, they wanted to go sailing. I always made sure Andy took his cell phone with him. He tried to call me."

Caroline felt her heart constrict. She'd heard this story. Not this version, exactly, but the same set of circumstances. Two best friends had gone sailing. Only one of them returned.

How could she tell Tori that now?

"Andy was frantic. God. He was barely thirteen. He went in after Brian. But Brian had gone under and Andy couldn't find him. He swam back to the boat and he called me. Me. He dialed my number because he didn't know what else to do."

"There isn't a word in the English language powerful enough to convey how horrible that must have been for you, for all of you, Tori."

Again, it was as if Tori hadn't heard. Staring straight ahead at the current flowing gently along the channel, she said, "I heard my cell phone ringing."

Tori became quiet. Too quiet.

"And?" Caroline asked. "You didn't answer?"

Her laugh filled with self-derision, Tori said, "I was a little busy."

Caroline knew it was too late to turn back now. Bad feeling or not, she said, "In what way?"

"I was having mind-altering sex."

"You mean you and Shane?"

"No. We were divorced by then. It was just some man I'd been seeing. I figured I'd get the message and return the call when we were finished, you know? Andy left me a voice mail. I'll never forget my baby's message. He was sobbing and panicked. He'd just seen his best friend drown. He needed his mother. Can you imagine how he must have felt, sailing that boat back to shore? Alone?" Tori's voice rose to near-hysteria. "And I didn't take the call until, well, you can imagine." Finally, she turned and looked at Caroline. "I wasn't there when he needed me."

"You've been there every day since."

"Obviously, that's not enough, is it?" She looked at the water again. "I think he figured out what I was doing. Who I was with. He hates me. And do you know what, Caroline? I don't blame him."

"My God." Caroline didn't know what else to say. *Everyone makes mistakes* seemed too simple; *it'll all work out* seemed terribly naive. "Don't a lot of teenagers say things like that?"

"It was a first for Andy."

Caroline felt a little like she did when she agreed to take a difficult case. She had to sort through everything that had been said, and in the process try to discern what hadn't been said. "Do you have any idea what instigated his outburst tonight?" she asked quietly.

Instead of replying, Tori stood. "I have to go."

"Tori, wait."

"I can't. Do you need a lift back to the summerhouse?"

"I can walk, but Tori —"

Tori was already hurrying away.

"Where are you going?" Caroline asked, rising, too.

"To find Andy. I've been pushing and

pushing and pushing him to make new friends. I'm only pushing him away. I have to tell him I was wrong. Two years ago. And this summer."

"I'll go with you," Caroline said.

Tori shook her head. In that instant she looked far older than thirty-seven. "I have to do this alone."

"All right, Tori. I'll call Pattie, Nell and Elaine. We'll be at my place. Call any one of us if you need anything. We'll be waiting."

Tori left. And Caroline was left sitting under the hundred-year-old Hickory Tree, thinking it had all been too easy, her friendships, her relationship with Shane, her new life.

Tori was wounded so deeply, Caroline couldn't even imagine how she would feel when she learned about this relationship between Caroline and Shane. What were the chances her first friend in Harbor Woods would turn out to have once been married to the man Caroline had fallen in love with? What were the chances she would have become pregnant in the first place? Or that she would discover the clues that would bring her here? What were the chances Henry O'Shaughnessy's death would stir up so many questions, or that the answers would be so far-reaching?

Tori still didn't know the half of it. Caroline never should have slept with Shane until she'd talked to Tori. Shane would have waited. That entire family was hurting, and Caroline was only making things worse.

Could she be any worse at relationships?

Slinging her bag over her shoulder, she walked home. She waited until she got there to call her friends. Pattie's husband Dave said she'd already left for the movies. She called both Pattie's and Nell's cell phones, and left a message on each of them. Elaine wasn't home, either.

Caroline paced as she waited.

It was liable to be a long night.

Shane was watching television in the dark when the knock sounded on the cruiser's hull.

"It's me, Shane. Dan Mitchell."

There were several reasons the local sheriff might pay him an unannounced visit after midnight. Every one of them scared the spit out of Shane.

He was up on deck before Dan finished coming aboard.

"It's Andy." By the time Dan said, "He's all right, or at least he's going to be," a hole had blown through Shane's left ventricle.

Okay. Andy was going to be all right. Breathe.

Damn.

Shane ran his hands down his chest, settling them on the waistband of his jeans. The sheriff was here. And Andy was going to be all right. What did that mean? Andy was in jail? No. Juvie? Impossible. He rarely went out.

"Where is he?"

"He's at the hospital getting stitched up."

Shane started for the pier, only to stop and backtrack for his shirt and shoes.

"Shane, wait."

Something in Dan's tone sent another kind of fear through Shane. Dan wasn't in uniform. Balding now, he'd thrown on some clothes haphazardly. They'd been on the same baseball team when they were kids. They'd attended each other's weddings and had gone fishing in the old days. The Mitchells held a barbecue every summer. Shane, Vickie and Andy used to go every year. After Shane's divorce, Dan and Sharon both assured him nothing would change. But everything always changed.

It had been Dan who'd come to the marina the day they'd found Brian. He was a decent man, and a good sheriff, which was why, when he told Shane to wait, Shane waited.

"There was an accident," Dan said, running a hand down his fleshy face. "A car accident."

"Andy was involved in a car accident? With Vickie?"

"No."

"A pedestrian accident? Someone hit him?"

"Apparently he was driving."

The right ventricle blew. Shane staggered. "Andy hasn't taken driver's ed. He's barely fifteen. He doesn't have his driver's license."

"Yes, we know. One of my deputies is waiting to talk to him right now. Off the record, if he were my son, I'd call an attorney."

The horrors just kept coming. Through it all, Shane heard himself say, "Was he alone?"

Dan shook his head.

Shane didn't recognize his own voice as he said, "Are the others —"

"They were alive. The last I knew."

Later, Shane wouldn't recall the drive to the hospital. He arrived fully clothed, so he must have gone below for his shirt and shoes. He was a mile away from his destination before he remembered Dan's advice regarding an attorney. By rote, he took out his cell phone and punched in Caroline's number.

She answered on the first ring.

"It's Shane. Are you still out with your friends?"

"No." Caroline had been pacing. Tori hadn't returned her calls. Elaine, Nell and Pattie hadn't heard from her, either. Caroline was feeling frantic.

"Can you come to the hospital?"

A dozen scenarios flashed through her head. "What happened? Are you hurt?"

"It's not me. It's Andy. He's in trouble, Caroline."

In the background she heard a voice over the intercom calling some doctor to E.R. "Which hospital?" Caroline asked.

"County Memorial. In Charlevoix."

"I'll be there in ten minutes."

The call was disconnected.

Caroline stopped, her feet rooted in place. The night just kept getting worse.

Thankfully, her professional demeanor kicked in. She located her keys and started her car on the first try. She drove within the speed limit. Barely. When her phone rang again, she placed it to her ear and calmly said, "Yes?"

"Caroline, there are eight voice mails from you."

"Tori?" It didn't sound like Tori.

"Yeah, it's me. Is everything all right with the baby?"

"Yes."

There was silence on both ends.

And then Caroline said, "What about you? Did you talk to Andy?" For all Caroline knew, Tori hadn't been told about the accident yet.

Tori broke down, and the sound cracked the outer edges of Caroline's professional demeanor. "Where are you?"

"I'm at the hospital," Tori whispered. "I need you to come."

"I'm on my way."

"I knew I could count on you."

Tori couldn't have realized that Caroline was literally already on her way. Caroline was put in mind of the first time she'd assisted Sheila Ross in an extremely difficult case. Just before springing a surprise on the unsuspecting opposition, meticulous, proper and hard-as-nails Sheila had muttered under her breath, "Stand back, ladies and gentlemen. The shit is about to hit the fan."

Tonight, Caroline couldn't stand back. In this instance, she was going to walk directly into the foray. In a matter of minutes, Tori would realize the connection between Caroline and Shane. She and Shane both needed her. Caroline couldn't let either of them down.

The parking lot was well lit and contained a large number of cars. Shane and Tori weren't among the people milling about the E.R. waiting room. Going directly to the desk, Caroline discreetly informed the nurse that she was an attorney and was here to speak with the Grady family. The kindly nurse led her past the area where Caroline had been examined several weeks ago.

"Your attorney's here," the other woman said, rapping softly on a closed door.

"Come in," Shane said from inside.

Professional mask in place, Caroline opened the door and went in. The room was small, the artificial lighting stark. There were the usual chrome-and-stainless-steel fixtures and sterile smell. Caroline was more interested in the three people looking at her.

"Thank God you're here," Shane said.

"That was fast," Tori said at the same time.

Since Tori didn't pick up on the coincidence, Caroline spared a glance at Andy. He was wearing a hospital gown. The head of the bed was raised, and a sheet covered him to his waist. There was a bandage on his forehead just above his eyebrow.

"Does that hurt?" she asked.

He met her gaze briefly, very briefly, then averted his face. "I already told the deputy what happened. I don't feel like repeating myself."

"You talked to the deputy without representation?" Caroline said. "Did he ask if you wanted it?"

"I don't think so. What difference does it make?"

"For God's sakes, Andy," Shane admonished. "It makes a lot of difference. I asked Caroline to come here to help."

"*You* asked her?" Tori said. "What do you mean you asked her? I just called her not more than —" She broke off in midsentence, as if something just clicked. In a blink, her entire countenance changed. "You two know each other?"

Shane said, "Yes."

Caroline said nothing, an answer that wasn't well received by either of them.

"No wonder you made such good time, Caroline. You were already on your way." Tori Young could be snide with the best of them.

Sparing another glance at Andy, Caroline said, "Let's deal with this problem now and sort out the other situation later, shall we?"

Tori glanced at Andy, too. "This is the

woman you thought was chunky." And to Caroline, "He's the guy with the beard. Well, isn't this cozy?" She started for the door.

"Mom, are you leaving?"

Her son's question stopped Tori in her tracks. Facing him, she said, "I'm going to find that deputy who talked to you without my authorization. Hopefully he hasn't left the hospital, because he's going to need medical attention when I'm finished with him." She looked back at Caroline, and then at Shane, and again at Andy. "I'm not leaving the hospital without you," she said. "You can bank on that."

While the click of Tori's heels grew fainter, Caroline closed the door, turning once again to the situation at hand. Shane looked like death. She would have liked to say something to ease his burden, but she focused her attention on Andy, and got down to business.

"Let's start at the beginning. In your own words, what happened?"

Caroline couldn't have been the only one fighting the need to massage her temples.

An hour ago, Tori had returned with the offending deputy in tow. Sheepishly, he'd admitted that he'd forgotten to obtain the proper authorization to question Andy, who was a minor. Caroline would make certain anything Andy had told him was rendered insubmissible in court, if the situation went that far.

Whether he wanted to or not, Andy had to begin again without the deputy present. His own words were sparse, but according to him, he'd willingly and knowingly gotten behind the wheel of an older boy's car. Evidently, the others had been drinking, but Andy hadn't. He hadn't offered this information. It was in the police report Caroline demanded to see.

They'd given Andy a Breathalyzer at the scene. There wasn't so much as a trace of alcohol in him. Thank God for that, at least.

Although the details were sketchy, Andy lost control and wrapped the car around a tree. Caroline would have to see the car. For now, she settled for viewing pictures. The only part of the car unscathed was the back door on the passenger side. The rest of the vehicle was mutilated, with the worst damage on the driver's door.

A nurse entered to check Andy's vitals and bandages. His right ankle was swollen. They wanted to keep him for a few hours, at least, for they suspected he had a slight concussion.

"All right, Andy," Caroline said.

Everyone looked at her.

"What do you mean all right?" Tori demanded.

"This is all I need from him right now. Perhaps he would like to rest now. I'd like to speak with the others involved."

Andy's gaze darted nervously to Caroline before sliding away. Shane saw it, too. Without saying a word, he accompanied Caroline from the room.

At the elevator, he said, "What do you think?"

She allowed herself only one glance at his face. She wouldn't have wanted to be him: the father of the boy to blame for an accident that had involved four other teenagers, two of whom were in serious condition.

"I'd like to speak to the others before I venture to say what I think happened."

The corridor on the second floor was full of family members of the other teens. Caroline learned that one of the boys, Jason Schuler, was in surgery to close a head wound and set a compound fracture in his left leg. His girlfriend, who'd also been in the car, had been examined and released. Caroline noted her crutches. Although the other boy was in less serious condition than

Jason, Caroline wasn't allowed to see him, either.

While Shane dealt with the shock, horror and blame in the parents' eyes, Caroline noticed another teenaged girl sitting by herself at the end of the corridor.

"Hi," Caroline said as she approached.

The girl's mascara was smeared, her face and arms scratched. She didn't appear to be seriously injured.

"It's two in the morning. You probably noticed I'm going to have a baby. Mind if I sit down?"

The girl inched over. Caroline took a seat. The girl remained huddled in her chair as far away as she could get.

"I'm a friend of Andy's family."

"I heard you were his attorney."

Caroline had to learn that news traveled fast in small towns. "I'm Caroline Moore. I *am* an attorney, but I'm not their attorney, per se."

"What does *per se* mean anyway?"

"It means by, of, in itself, or as such."

Pretty, hopelessly young and scantily clad in a flimsy little top held up by spaghetti straps, the girl made a sound by releasing her breath through her pursed lips. It was short for *It was a rhetorical question, stupid.*

Well then.

"Which one is your boyfriend?" Caroline asked.

The girl sniffled. "Chris. He's not hurt as bad as Jason. Danielle's a real basket case."

"Are your parents coming for you?"

The girl sniffled again. "They're out of town. They're going to kill me. I'm staying with Danielle this week. Her parents are over there."

Clearly, the girl didn't want to talk to Caroline.

"If it's any consolation," Caroline said as if oblivious, "if Jason's injuries were more serious, they would have airlifted him to a larger facility."

"Really?"

Caroline nodded.

"You're saying people don't die here?"

So much for putting the girl's mind at ease. Suddenly, Caroline understood why parents of teenagers worried. They were smart, sometimes reckless, untrusting of adults and they stuck together.

"I saw pictures of the car."

The girl made no move to reply.

"You must have been sitting in the middle in the back."

"So?"

"Chris was on your left. That side of the

car took the brunt of the impact with the tree."

"That's what they tell *me*."

"I'd rather you tell me."

"Tell you what?"

"Tell me how Andy Grady could have possibly been driving?"

"What do you mean?"

"If he'd been driving," Caroline said, laying a hand gently on the girl's arm, "Andy would be the one in surgery right now."

The girl — Caroline had yet to learn her name — wouldn't meet Caroline's gaze. Mumbling something about wanting to sit with her friends, she got up, leaving Caroline without a backward glance.

Caroline watched her. She said something to the other girl involved. A private conference followed. Eventually, they both nodded, falling silent.

By then, Tori and Shane were waiting for Caroline near the elevators. Meeting them there, she said, "I believe I've gathered enough information for now. I think I'll go home."

"You're not coming?" Shane asked.

Caroline had to give Tori credit for refraining from rolling her eyes.

"I'm sure you'd both like to stay with Andy."

"Well?" Tori was finally forced to ask. "What do you think about Andy's story?"

"He wasn't driving that car."

"Somebody told you that?" Again, it was Tori who'd spoken.

Shane's attention never wavered from Caroline's face.

"No one *admitted* it," Caroline said. "But that girl I just talked to knows it. They all do. I'll be able to prove it from the photographs of the car and the injuries sustained by those involved."

"Christ, you sound like a lawyer," Tori grumbled. "You're saying Andy's lying."

"From what you've told me, Tori — and Shane —" it was as close as Caroline came to their other situation "— Andy may have a death wish, but I don't believe he would have jeopardized anyone else's life."

"Then why is he taking the blame?" Shane asked.

"Because he wants to be punished." Tori stared at Caroline as if daring her to say that he came by that naturally.

"Normally," Caroline said instead, "formal charges are filed in these situations. Since Andy confessed, he'll likely be charged. They'll be dropped eventually. If you'd like, I'll represent him. Pro bono."

Tori's only reply was a curt nod. The

elevator opened with a small ding. She got in. Without a word, she rode it back down to the E.R.

Caroline and Shane were still in plain view of the other families. It was very late and tensions were high. Shane looked it. His gaze rested on hers. Although he didn't smile, probably couldn't, his expression softened and he seemed to breathe a little easier.

"I don't know where to begin to thank you. It was awkward for you earlier."

"I think it was hardest on Tori."

"It might take her a little while to get used to the fact that we're seeing each other, but I still don't see why our relationship should bother her. It has nothing to do with her."

Caroline didn't want to talk about Tori behind her back. Nor would she betray a confidence. Therefore, she said nothing. But Caroline knew her relationship with Shane bothered Tori. She wasn't quite certain of all the reasons, but Andy was at the heart of them. Or perhaps it was Tori herself who was at the heart of everything she was facing. Caroline thought about some of the things Tori had told her in confidence earlier. Tori blamed herself for that day two years ago. There had to be something Caroline was missing. In every situation, there was always more. Look at Caroline's life. Look at Anna's, and Karl's.

Shane squeezed her hand. They both rode the next elevator to the main floor. There, he retraced his footsteps to Andy's hospital room and Caroline headed for the exit.

CHAPTER 16

Caroline opened her eyes and tried to get her bearings. The sun was coming up. That must have meant it was morning.

She tried to get out of bed, but instead of finding the edge of the mattress, she encountered the back of the sofa. Why was she on the sofa?

Her brain wasn't working very efficiently. In order to get up, she was going to have to roll over. That wasn't as easy as it used to be, either.

She wondered what had awakened her. One by one, last night's events came back to her: the phone calls, the drive to the hospital, and then the details of the accident. Hoping to hear from Tori or Shane, she'd waited on the sofa for one or both of them to call. Neither had.

A car door slammed. It was five forty-five in the morning. Whoever it was, wasn't making a social call.

Shane arrived at her front door at the same time she did. She'd slept in her clothes. It didn't look as if he'd slept at all. Without saying a word, he came in, closing the door behind him. There was a span of time during which neither of them moved. And then they walked straight into each other's arms.

She didn't know how long they stood that way, not speaking, simply holding on. Finally, she said, "I take it they released Andy?"

"He was asleep in his own bed when I left Vickie's. Hell."

Caroline could only imagine how that had gone. Yawning, she padded to the kitchen to put the coffee on. He took over, shooing her to the bar stool where he'd sat a few months ago when he'd first told her about his son. She wasn't accustomed to being taken care of. She'd heard of the existence of men in her generation who saw to a woman's needs, but until Shane, she'd never experienced one personally. Shane might not have wanted to admit it, but he took care of people. Or he tried.

It would be easy to want more.

Her feelings for him went deep. He was good-looking but not gorgeous. And he was missing his socks again. It wasn't his appearance that made him unique. Nor was it the fact that his hair and beard needed a trim and he rarely wore socks. There was inherent goodness in him. He wasn't perfect, far from it in fact, but he was one of the good guys, probably one of those saints Tori had once said she didn't want.

He should have been dead on his feet, and yet he moved with an economy of motion, easily and efficiently as if loose-jointed. On land or on the water, rested or in dire need of sleep, the man was dangerous. She'd known it the first time they'd met.

They'd grown quiet again. Quietude never bothered him. She found she liked that about him, too.

When the coffeemaker stopped hissing, he poured the steaming brew into two mugs. Next, he poured her a glass of orange juice. Making no attempt to hide the fact that he was watching her, he waited until she'd taken her first sip before he said, "Small world, huh?"

It wasn't funny. "Don't make light of it, Shane. Just don't."

Shane had heard this speech before. From the other side of the kitchen island, he leaned down. Resting his elbows on the countertop so that he and Caroline were at eye level, he said, "By now you know I'm not good at *don't*."

He wanted to twine his fingers through hers, to hold her hand. That wasn't all he wanted, but he would have settled for it right now. Instead, he took another slurp of decaf and said, "I don't know if this is the time or the place, but I said it before and I'll say it again. Vickie and I have been divorced for four years. She could tell you the exact number of days, hours and minutes. Our marriage shriveled up and died long before she filed the papers. You're the first woman I've wanted to see since. I realize it's the mother of all coincidences. But Caroline? Vickie doesn't take friendship lightly. She'll get used to you and me."

"You really don't know anything about women, do you?"

"I know I don't want to lose you." He took her hand then. "And I know we're both dead on our feet. Come on. There's no place either of us has to go for a few hours, at least."

Leaving their steaming coffee on the counter, he led her to her bed. And he lay down with her, he on his back, she on her side, her head on his chest, the weight of her belly resting lightly against him.

"If your offer to represent Andy still

stands, Vickie and I would appreciate your expertise."

"Of course it stands. I'll speak with the sheriff and the prosecuting attorney later this morning. Would the three of you be able to come by my office this afternoon?"

"What time?"

"Let's say three o'clock."

Placing two fingers beneath her chin, he tilted her face up slightly. Her eyes were hooded and as blue as the morning. She expected him to kiss her. He wanted to. But one kiss would most likely lead to another. So instead he drew the sheet over her shoulders.

Two minutes later, they were both sound asleep.

Caroline expected the meeting to be awkward. From the onset, it was all of that and more.

Upon hearing the bell jangle over the door, she greeted Shane, Tori and Andy in the outer office. Shane looked worried, Tori looked downright hostile. Andy didn't meet Caroline's eyes.

"This way," she said.

She led them into her inner office where three chairs were arranged opposite her desk. She remained standing until they were all inside. Andy came bumping in on crutches. Tori followed, and finally Shane closed the door.

While they got situated in the chairs, Andy in the middle, his father on his right, his mother on his left, Caroline busied herself with paperwork at Karl's old desk. The moment they were seated, she sat, too. "This won't take long. I have good news. The charges have been dropped, just as I expected."

"Thank God," Tori said, only to clamp her mouth shut because her little outburst gave Caroline the perfect excuse to look at her.

"Amen to that," Caroline said. She couldn't help offering her friend a small smile. She wasn't surprised it wasn't reciprocated.

"What happens next?" Tori asked, sticking to business.

Caroline pushed several papers across her desk. "There are forms for you to sign. The top one is a copy of the charges. The next one is a copy of the police report. Last is the paperwork stating that the charges have been dropped. I need all three of your signatures on that one, but just your initials on the first two for my files. If you'd like to read them first, by all means do so."

While Tori scanned the legalese, Caroline turned to Andy. The wound above his eyebrow had bled through the bandage slightly. His eye was swollen and on its way to a full-fledged shiner. "You're lucky, Andy. All five of you kids are lucky."

He looked away.

Normally, she gave a client who'd lied to her a firm lecture. Knowing what she knew about Andy Grady's situation, she opted to forgo it this time. After all, there was nothing she could tell him about guilt he didn't already feel.

Tori signed the forms then handed them to Andy, who scribbled his name hurriedly before passing them on to his dad. When Shane had finished, Caroline took them from him. "Justin Schuler is out of danger. He admitted he was driving. The police are attributing the mix-up to shock."

Shane ran his hand through his shaggy hair and sighed loud enough for all of them to hear.

"Does anyone have any questions?" Caroline asked.

Tori shook her head. Andy looked down. And Shane stared directly into Caroline's eyes.

After making copies of the first two forms, and tearing off the bottom copy of the documents stating that the charges had been dropped, Caroline handed a set to Tori and another to Shane. Next, Caroline stood, indicating that the meeting was over.

"That's it?" Andy asked before he could help himself.

Caroline's smile was genuine. "It hardly seems worth all the trouble it took you to hobble down here, does it?"

"It was worth all the trouble and more," Shane said, speaking for the first time. "Andy, I believe you have something to say."

So softly he was nearly inaudible, Andy mumbled, "I'm sorry."

With an almost imperceptible shake of her head at Shane, Caroline said, "We'll just chalk it up to experience."

This time it was Tori whose sigh was heard throughout the room. She stood, too, handing Andy his crutches.

When his son had hoisted himself to his good leg, Shane said, "Andy is going to pay you for your time."

The other three wore expressions of equal surprise.

Resigning himself to the situation, Andy said, "I'll take it out of savings."

"That really isn't necessary," Caroline said. "I would rather see you put that money toward your education."

"Good idea," Shane said. Before the other three could breathe sighs of relief, he said, "He'll work it off."

"He'll what?" Tori asked.

"He can work it off."

"Doing what?" Caroline and Tori asked at the same time.

"Doing odd jobs for Ms. Moore," Shane said. "That agreeable to you, Andy?"

The boy shrugged. "I guess."

Shane was on a roll. "Your mother and I have made arrangements for you to start talking to a counselor."

"About what?" Andy said, louder now.

"That's entirely up to you." The tone of Shane's voice left no room for argument.

Shane could tell Caroline wanted to say something. Vickie's eyes shot daggers at him. Tough. Sometimes things had to get worse before they could get better. Maybe last night had been rock bottom. At least he and Vickie were finally on the same page regarding the teen psychiatrist. She'd been right about that. Maybe someday he would tell her so.

Shane had asked Paul Avery for his opinion regarding Andy's method of repaying Caroline for her help. Dr. Avery agreed that working off a debt was often instrumental in relieving guilt and self-blame. Shane didn't know what it would take to relieve his son's guilt over his best friend's death. Perhaps nothing would, but at least this was a start.

Finally, things were looking up. It had been a long time since Shane had felt as if happiness was actually remotely possible. Caroline had a lot to do with that.

With utmost professionalism, she was seeing them to the door. Even in business attire, she looked maternal now. Shane happened to know there was more to her than either her professional facade or her maternal persona. Behind closed doors, she was sensual, earthy, ardent and so damned responsive he could get worked up again a day later just thinking about it.

"Thank you, Ms. Moore," Andy said, exiting the door Tori was holding.

"You're welcome, Andy."

"Are you free for dinner tonight?" Shane asked.

He could tell from Caroline's expression that she didn't believe this was the time or the place. She might have thought she could end this meeting without broaching anything personal. Shane wasn't about to let it go at that. He'd asked in front of Vickie intentionally.

He wanted the awkwardness behind them.

He was sick and tired of it, of all of it.

"I can't," Caroline said quietly. "Tonight's girls' night. Isn't it, Tori?"

"Same time, same place," Tori said with little inflection as she followed Andy out the door.

It was no coincidence that Caroline was the last to arrive. She knew what she was in for, and she was ready.

Taking her usual seat at Tori's kitchen table, she said, "Sorry I'm late. I took a long nap."

"From what I hear, you deserved it," Elaine said.

Caroline wasn't sure how much Tori had told the others, if she'd told them anything.

"The accident was on the news," Nell said, scooping ice cream into parfait glasses.

Was Caroline an open book these days?

"Receiving that dreaded, middle-of-the-night knock on the door is every parent's worst nightmare," Nell said, patting Tori's hand.

"Thank God those kids are going to be okay," Elaine countered conversationally. "Now that we've satisfied that topic, you're seeing Shane?"

Caroline measured the women in the room. Tori's face was well modeled and carefully expressionless. Elaine's bangs hid her forehead, but not her open dismay. Nell seemed to have forgotten about the ice cream. Then there was Pattie, the resident diplomat and in many ways the woman most like Caroline. Even pleasant, happily married Pattie, who was normally every-one's ally, was waiting with bated breath.

Accepting the inevitable, Caroline said, "I met Shane my first day in Harbor Woods. I didn't know he was Tori's ex-husband until much later. One of you called Tori's ex Grady. I assumed that was his first name. And Tori's last name is Young. And he calls his ex-wife Vickie. Looking back, I should have seen the clues."

"Such as?" Elaine asked.

Caroline spoke to Tori. "You both called your son Andy."

"That's not an uncommon name," Nell said.

"You both told me he was fifteen."

"A lot of kids are fifteen," Nell insisted.

"Would you mind?" Tori grumbled. Next, she turned to Caroline. "You never men-tioned Shane's name, either. Like the time you told me you'd kissed some guy who had a beard."

"You told Tori you kissed a man, and

neither of you knew you were referring to her ex?"

Everyone shot Nell a quelling look.

"Just pointing out the irony."

"How did you meet Shane?" Tori asked.

"I was looking for Karl Peterson. Shane's mother told me to talk to Shane, and sent me to the marina."

"It figures." Tori made a derogatory sound. "What did Karl have to do with you?"

"He was my grandfather."

Four women leaned ahead on their elbows. Everyone shut up and listened. Even Nell.

CHAPTER 17

Caroline began at the beginning, when she'd discovered the letter in her grandfather's attic in Lake Forest. Briefly, she told Elaine, Nell, Pattie and Tori what the letter said and how it insinuated that Caroline's mother hadn't been Henry O'Shaughnessy's biological child.

Looking at each of them in turn, she said, "I was at loose ends in Chicago. I thought the last of my family had died. When I discovered there may have been another branch of my family tree, I had to come here to find out if it was true. I'd hoped Karl was still healthy and coherent. He was neither, and yet I learned the most interesting things about his childhood and his life."

"Did he know you or recognize you?" Nell asked.

Caroline touched a lock of her hair. "I don't think he knew who I was, but now I wonder if sometimes he might have thought

I was Anna."

"So Anna and Karl were lovers when they were young," Elaine said.

"All three of them were close. I don't know if Anna knew it, but both men loved her. By the time Anna realized she was pregnant, Karl had shipped out and she couldn't reach him. People didn't have many options back then. Henry offered her a chance to have an honorable life. He married her, and gave my mother his name. In the letter she said she was lucky to have been loved by two men. She wondered if they were as lucky to have been loved by her. Anna died when my mother was a little girl. And Henry raised Elsa by himself."

"So," Pattie said, wiping melting ice cream off the table, "Karl never knew he'd fathered a child?"

"Oh, he knew. Shane found a letter Karl had hidden in the lighthouse. It was the letter Anna wrote informing Karl she'd married Henry. She told him she was sorry, and that she'd had no other choice. I'm sure Karl read between those lines."

"How can you be so sure?" Elaine asked.

Caroline noticed that Tori wasn't talking.

She understood why girls' night usually wound up here. Tori had a knack for making a person feel comfortable and at home.

Her kitchen contained just the right amount of party clutter. Uncorked wine bottles stood beside stemware and fresh flowers and cheese and fruit trays. There were sweets for Nell and spicy dip for Elaine and chips for Pattie. Normally there was bottled water for Caroline, but she didn't see any tonight.

She recalled the first time she'd met these four women. It had been Tori who'd invited her, but they'd all accepted her, each in her own unique way. By her very nature, Caroline was guarded and often private. She was learning that an important element of friendship was trust. Elaine had said it that first night. *What was said here stayed here.* Perhaps this was the test of true friendship.

"Because after Karl's funeral, Shane and I found a stack of newspaper clippings in Karl's house. I was featured in every one, from my birth announcement to piano recitals to college graduation, all the way to newsworthy cases I won."

"If you're Karl's granddaughter, why haven't you come forward with it? People here would snap that up," Nell insisted.

Caroline said, "Karl didn't tell anyone. And I don't feel it's my place to do so. It's enough that I know he knew."

"That halo must get tight." Finally, something from Tori.

"How long have you and Shane been an item?"

"We started out as friends because of Karl."

"Are you sleeping with him?" Tori asked point-blank.

Caroline wasn't the only one who gasped.

Sharing personal information with her friends was one thing. Her sex life was private. "What difference would that make?"

"It matters to me. Are you?"

"Would I still be welcome at girls' night if I were?" Caroline asked.

"I'm not the only person who would decide that." Digging in her heels, Tori said, "Would you stop seeing him if I asked you to?"

Elaine, Nell and Pattie might as well have been watching a tennis match.

"Would you if the situation were reversed?" Caroline asked.

Nell nearly choked on her ice cream.

Caroline looked around the room. She and Tori seemed to have reached an impasse. This was Tori's home, this group of friends and their weekly get-togethers her doing.

Tonight had been a test of friendship. It was too soon to know if she'd passed.

"I have one more question," Tori insisted. "If your relationship with Shane is so damn innocent, why didn't you tell anybody about it?"

Caroline didn't have anything to say to that. She'd tried to tell Tori. Even now Caroline knew how weak that would sound. Caroline hadn't planned her relationship with Shane. She certainly hadn't planned to fall in love with him. The situation wasn't cut-and-dried. There were extenuating circumstances. And yet Caroline knew she should have offered Tori the same thing Tori offered all of them.

Honesty.

"I'm sorry," she said. And she meant it. No one seemed to know what to say.

With quiet dignity, Caroline bid everyone a good-night.

Wasn't this just peachy, Tori thought snidely after Caroline left.

"One thing I've noticed about Caroline," Elaine said. "She knows how to make an exit."

Tori grunted a reply.

No matter how covert they were trying to be, she noticed the glances the other three cast one another. They let the subject drop. Tori appreciated their sensitivity and discretion. It didn't do anything to alleviate the ugliness at the core of her. It went so deep no plastic surgeon's scalpel could reach it. Tori didn't know what to do about it. She never had.

"Caroline! Look at you," Elaine exclaimed. "You've bloomed."

Tears gathered in Caroline's eyes. She could hardly believe how good it was to see Elaine.

She hadn't been back to girls' night. This would be the third consecutive week she'd missed. Nell and Pattie had stopped by the summerhouse last week and again yesterday. Today, Elaine was here to talk about her imminent divorce.

Taking a seat in her inner office, Caroline said, "Yesterday Pattie told me I've popped. I prefer your terminology."

"The last trimester is always the most uncomfortable. It's good to see you. I read about you in the local paper. Former Chicago Attorney Makes Harbor Woods New Home. That was good publicity."

"Free publicity," Caroline said. "Thanks to Shane, who has a friend at the paper."

Elaine met Caroline's eyes. "How is Shane?"

"He's Shane." But she smiled, and somehow she had a feeling that said it all. She and Shane spent most nights together during the week when Andy wasn't staying with his father. Shane had offered to fill in for Tori in her parenting classes, but Caroline went alone.

She hadn't called Elaine in to discuss her relationship with Shane, and nothing new had developed between her and Tori. She'd been officially open for business for a week. Off his crutches now, Andy had given all the walls a fresh coat of paint. Shane believed his son was making progress. The boy could do almost anything. He was polite to a fault. Too polite. Caroline wasn't sure she agreed with Shane. She hadn't called Elaine in to discuss Andy, either.

"I believe I've discovered a loophole in your prenup," Caroline said.

"You have?"

"It's about the size of the eye of a needle, but I've won cases for clients on less."

Elaine leaned ahead. "I'm listening."

Caroline outlined her plan. She referenced every legal document, bank statement and tax form Elaine had supplied. Citing other cases, she said, "I can prove you helped Justin build at least two of his businesses, both of which were started after your marriage. That's our loophole, the *i* that wasn't dotted. If you decide to proceed, we'll have to move quickly, freezing his assets, tying his hands, so to speak, so he can't transfer funds or hide figures in any way, shape or form. Be forewarned. This isn't going to be pretty. And his attorneys will go for our jugulars."

"Will it be worth it, Caroline?"

"I believe it's worth it to get you what you deserve. I don't feel we'll gain anything by attempting to give Justin what he deserves. As long as we leave vindication out of it and remain focused on what you've accomplished for the businesses, not on the affairs Justin has had, I believe we'll come out ahead."

By the time Caroline showed Elaine to the door, they'd outlined a plan.

"Next stop is my hairstylist's," Elaine said. "I'm biting the bullet and going short. You may not want vindication, but I do. Justin hates short hair."

Noting the expression of satisfaction in her friend's eyes, Caroline said, "I'm going to have to drive to Charlevoix tomorrow to see the new you."

"You could come to girls' night instead."

"I miss you, too, Elaine, but I don't think Tori's ready for that."

"I don't understand her. Nobody understands her."

That, Caroline thought as Elaine left her office in downtown Harbor Woods, was the problem.

Caroline made sure Tori's car was in the parking lot before she ventured into the real estate office in Charlevoix. The receptionist smiled the way all receptionists did when greeting potential clients. "May I help you?"

"I'm here to see Tori Young."

"Do you have an appointment?"

And give Tori the opportunity to refuse to see her? Caroline didn't think so. "I'm afraid not. Does she have a few minutes free?"

The receptionist scanned the screen of her computer. "I believe she does."

Caroline felt a little sorry for the reprimand the unsuspecting receptionist was going to receive from Tori for this. Pushing a button on the intercom, she said, "There's someone here to see you, Tori."

"Who?"

I'll take it from here, Caroline mouthed, already on her way to Tori's office.

"It's me, Tori," she said, opening the door.

She entered without waiting for an invitation.

Tori's eyes widened and then narrowed slightly. "What brings you to Charlevoix?"

"You look good. Is that a new suit?"

Tori shrugged.

And Caroline said, "My lease will be up on the summerhouse soon."

"I'm fairly certain the owner will be happy to extend it on a monthly basis."

"That's good to know," Caroline said, taking a seat. "Meanwhile I'd like to begin looking for a house to purchase."

Silence.

"I'd like you to be my buyer's agent. I also have my last parenting class tonight. Everyone's been asking about you."

"I figured Shane's been going with you."

"He hasn't. Do you still have feelings for Shane, Tori?"

"Don't be ridiculous."

"Then what issue are we dealing with here?"

"Please don't try to psychoanalyze me. It's bad enough you're seeing my ex-husband, who seems to be wrapped around your little finger. Now my son follows you around like a lovesick puppy. Don't get me wrong. I'm glad Andy is better. Of course, you've heard all about that."

Caroline wasn't going to pretend that Shane hadn't kept her apprised of the progress Andy was making in his outpatient therapy with Dr. Avery.

"I guess it's pretty tough on Andy," Tori

said, "but he's started to talk about Brian in therapy. And he likes *you*."

"He does?" Caroline asked.

"Of course he does."

This was news to her. "Andy works diligently at whatever task I give him, but he rarely says more than two-word sentences." Caroline watched Tori closely to see if she would gloat. She didn't.

Her intercom buzzed, and the receptionist informed her that her two-o'clock appointment was here.

Caroline's attempt to heal the rift in the friendship or even to make the slightest progress in that direction failed. As she left the real estate office, it occurred to her that getting anything out of Tori was as difficult as getting information out of her son. The two were alike. Maybe that was the problem. Or maybe therein lay the answer.

But what, exactly, was the question? Maybe Tori was right. Maybe it would be best if Caroline left the psychoanalyzing to the proper professionals.

Caroline was doing laundry on Saturday when Andy arrived. He'd been coming regularly these past few weeks and had nearly worked off his fee. She would have been happy to have called them even, but

Shane was adamant that Andy needed to pay it back in full, for his sake, as well as Caroline's.

When it came to what was best for Andy, Caroline never argued. She hadn't slept well. Who could sleep with a little foot pressed on her bladder all night? Placing a hand lovingly on her stomach, she opened the door. "Good morning."

"Hey," Andy said.

Stepping back to let him enter, she said, "Your dad says you're good with directions and blueprints and assembling things. Do you think you can figure out the proper assembly for the baby's crib?" She gestured to the parts littering the living-room floor. "Because I can't tell the difference between slot A and C or the left side and the right."

He got to work. And she returned to the amazingly tiny baby clothes she'd been folding when he arrived. Andy was extremely bright, and sensitive beyond belief. She wondered if it was possible he was what they called an Indigo Child in the child-development articles she'd been reading. Before she'd become pregnant, she would have dismissed the idea that some children were born with a special gift and an aura that appeared dark blue to people who claimed they could see auras. Now, she didn't dismiss anything as impossible. She questioned everything and she devoured all the literature she could find on the subject of parenting and child development.

She noticed Andy looking at her speculatively. "Something on your mind?" she asked, placing something called a onesy on top of a stack of sleepers.

He seemed embarrassed. Although they'd spent time together since the accident, they weren't easy around each other. Something was holding him back. When he returned to the crib assembly, she assumed he wasn't going to reply.

Out of the blue, he said, "Are you and my dad going to get married?"

She proceeded with caution. "We haven't talked about marriage. Your dad is a wonderful man. I've only known him for a few months."

"So it's not his kid?"

Ah. "No, Andy, it isn't his child."

She knew little about children, and even less about teenaged boys. She stared at him.

"What?" he asked.

"You just reminded me of someone."

"My dad?"

"No, your mother."

He dropped the parts he'd been trying to put together. "I wouldn't tell her that."

"Why?" she asked.

"She'd take it as an insult."

Caroline placed her hand at the small of her aching back. It was still hotter than blazes outside. Since when was September the hottest month of the summer? The idea of autumn beckoned.

"Your mom loves you. I never want to be caught in the middle of the two of you. I feel bad for —"

"I don't want sympathy."

"What do you want?" she asked.

"Maybe I want everybody to stop looking at me like I'm some kind of freak."

"Who looks at you as if you're a freak? Not me. I see a kid who looks like his father and acts like his mother. Maybe I *should* feel sorry for you for that, but I don't."

He stared at her. And then he did something completely unexpected. He smiled.

After today, Andy's debt would be paid in full. Caroline supposed it stood to reason it had taken them until now to reach an understanding. She doubted Tori was going to be pleased about that. In Tori's eyes, it would be one more way someone else had reached her child when she couldn't.

Caroline straightened suddenly. That was it. That was what was at the heart of the problem. Tori wasn't jealous of Caroline because of Shane. She was jealous because of Andy.

She finished folding a stack of tiny sleepers and was on her way to the little room Shane had helped her set up as a nursery, both hands full of baby items. Pain tore through her with so much force she doubled over.

She must have groaned, because Andy looked at her. "What's wrong?"

"I don't know."

"What do I do?"

It was all she could do to speak through the pain. "I think the baby's coming."

"Now? Here?" He started toward her only to stop at the sight of the blood seeping into the baby clothes she'd dropped.

CHAPTER 18

On the floor, Caroline lay curled in the fetal position. She could hear Andy talking.

He must have dialed 911. "No, she's not my mother. Who cares about that? She's in a hell of a lot of pain. She's going to have a kid and there's blood everywhere."

Caroline recognized his panic. But then another pain seared through her, consuming her. The next time she was aware of anything else, she heard Andy yelling into the phone. "Mom! She's bleeding. I can't do this."

She closed her eyes again, drifting in a place that obliterated every sound, every thought, everything except pain and fear. She didn't know how much time elapsed, but eventually she felt a hand on her forehead and then on her abdomen.

"Sweet Jesus."

It sounded like Tori. Somewhere, a phone was ringing. In the farthest reaches of Caroline's mind, she realized the 911 operator had called back.

"Fine," Tori was saying. "I'll stay on the line. You'll be here in how long? Twenty minutes? That's what you told my son three minutes ago." She used the most unbecoming word known to mankind. "It'll be too late by then. I said I'd stay on the line, didn't I? Andy," she said, "help me get Caroline into my car. Grab some towels, son. That's it."

Somehow they got Caroline into the back seat of Tori's SUV. "Don't worry." Tori dove into the driver's seat. "We'll get you to the hospital."

Andy climbed in beside Caroline, who was lying on the back seat. Crouching down, he said, "Mom, what do I do?"

"Just make sure she doesn't roll out of the seat." Tori must have picked up the phone. "I said I wouldn't hang up, didn't I? I'm bringing her to the hospital myself. We'll be there in five minutes. What?" And then, "Don't worry. You'll recognize me. We'll be the car doing ninety with our emergency flashers blazing. You tell them in E.R. they'd better have the best damn doctor on staff waiting at the door."

Lying in the back seat, Caroline could only moan. It wasn't supposed to be this way. It was too soon. She hadn't grown tired of being pregnant. Her baby was too small.

It was too soon.

The next aeon was a blur of bright lights and barking voices and movement. Caroline had been lifted from the back seat to a gurney. There was an elevator ride, and more pain, so intense, so searing she thought she would die from it. Once, she thought she had died, for there was one moment when the pain went away and she felt nothing, heard nothing, saw nothing.

Then another pain overtook her, and she knew death couldn't hurt this much, be this loud or this blindingly bright. She didn't know where she was. But Tori and Andy weren't with her.

It seemed someone was working on her at every end. An oxygen mask was placed over her face, an IV started in her arm, a blood-pressure monitor, somewhere. At the very center of her, pain, pain and pain.

She heard beeping and voices and someone yelling, "Push, Caroline."

She couldn't. She was too weak. And it hurt too much.

"Push. We've got to get your baby out now. Push."

She pushed.

And she screamed.

And she pushed again. And again.

At some point the pain subsided. She opened her eyes against the bright lights. And listened to the sounds of silence.

"What's happening?" she said through the oxygen mask.

"It's a girl," someone said.

There was a suction sound, and a frail squeak, and finally a whimper.

"Atta girl," somebody said. "Use those lungs."

"Caroline, look," a nurse said.

Caroline turned her head, and there was her baby being wrapped in a towel.

"Give me your hand."

The nurse placed Caroline's hand on her child's little torso. "You have a daughter."

Caroline smiled. She had a daughter. Seven weeks premature, she was tiny and skinny and pale, but she was warm, and she was breathing.

And there was hope.

Shane burst into the hospital like a wave breaking shore.

Andy jumped out of his chair. "Shit, Dad," he said. "Mom can drive!"

"From what I hear," Shane said, fighting tears of pride and humbleness and just about everything else, "you're both pretty damn good under pressure."

Andy glanced away, embarrassed, but proud, too. "Caroline's sleeping. Mom's sitting with her. They won't let anybody else in her room."

"And the baby?"

"Wait'll you see her. I used to catch fish bigger than she is."

Andy led the way to the elevators. Inside, he punched the proper button, and up they went. Shane's stomach stayed on the first floor. But his pride for the boy-man who was his son shot up to the fourth floor along with him.

He looked at Andy.

"What?"

Shane shook his head. "I was just thinking about time. Just the other day, I was going to the nursery to admire you."

"Fifteen years ago, you mean."

"That's what I said. Just the other day."

Caroline opened her eyes to bickering.

"I go fishing one day, and all hell breaks loose."

"I've been telling you for years you have to stop trying to keep all the balls in the air all the time."

"You never told me that."

"Fine."

Recognizing Shane's and Tori's voices, Caroline couldn't help smiling. "Have you seen her yet?"

Shane and Tori looked at her from opposite sides of her bed. She felt Shane's hand go around hers. "I went to see her when they wouldn't let me see you. Somebody was hogging the visitation rights."

"Just remember who got her here."

They were at it again.

"You should be glad I went to the trouble to contact you at all," Tori grumbled. "If I hadn't called the Coast Guard, you'd still be out there trying to snare some poor unsuspecting lunker salmon."

"How is she?" Caroline asked.

Shane seemed to come to his senses. Hunkering down so his face was close to Caroline's, he said, "She was sucking her thumb when Andy and I saw her a few minutes ago. She weighs four pounds and eleven ounces and she's already strong enough to suck her thumb. They're keeping a close watch on her, though. She's got an IV and oxygen, but they said she's a fighter. She has red hair, Caroline. I bet Karl's getting a kick out of that."

Caroline was getting lost in the way Shane was looking at her. Tori cleared her throat. "Guess I'll be going."

"Don't go," Caroline called. "I haven't thanked you. How do I, Tori?" A tear trailed into Caroline's hair.

"I didn't do anything anybody else wouldn't have done."

"Pardon my French, but that's bullshit and you know it."

Caroline had everyone's attention.

"Andy called *you*," Caroline said. "He needed *you*. And *you* were there. I guess you're just going to have to deal with it."

"You think you're so smart."

"I would have lost her if not for you and Andy. How is he, by the way?"

Tori shrugged. "He's taking all the credit. He's a man, all right. I think he's going to be okay."

"Are you ready to give me your permission, Tori?"

Tori made that sound she made through her tightly pursed lips. "Ha! Get some rest. Once you leave this hospital, you won't sleep again for the rest of your life." She looked at Caroline, then at Shane, and finally away.

"Tori?" Shane called.

She turned in the doorway. "That's my name, don't wear it out."

With a tilt of his head, he said, "Thanks."

"Yeah?"

"Yeah."

For the first time in years, the two of them smiled at each other. And meant it.

CHAPTER 19

Ahhhh. This was more like it. This beat hospital drab any day.

Tori took a sip of her margarita. The lights were dim. The music was loud. The club was crowded. And the Jude Law look-alike across the room couldn't take his eyes off her.

The emergency girls' night had been Nell's idea. Going to the club had been Tori's, but even Pattie, whose husband usually gave her grief about coming here, had agreed to the celebration. Of course, they'd all wanted to hear the entire story of Caroline's baby's birth, detail by infinitesimal detail.

"Andy hung up on the 911 operator to call you?"

"I heard that's a no-no. The kid has balls, Tori."

"Thank goodness, he was at Caroline's."

"You really drove ninety miles per hour?"

"And you beat the ambulance to the hospital?"

Tori had been doing a lot of nodding this evening. They'd met the ambulance halfway to the hospital. It had turned around and followed them, lights and sirens blaring the entire way.

"You and Andy saved Caroline's life and her baby's, too," Pattie said.

"I don't know about that," Tori said. "But we got her there in time for the doctors and medical staff to do their thing."

"You did more than that, and you know it," Elaine insisted.

"You deserve an award or some kind of medal." Nell took a sip of her strawberry daiquiri.

Caroline's words filtered through Tori's mind. *Andy called you. He needed you. And you were there. I guess you're just going to have to deal with it.*

She'd been dealing with it all day.

After leaving Caroline's hospital room, she'd gone downstairs to the lobby, where Andy was sitting by himself.

He'd looked up as she approached. "Hey," he'd said.

"Hey," she'd replied, taking the chair next to his.

They both leaned back, suddenly exhausted. "We make a pretty good team," she said.

"Yeah?"

"Yeah." She'd looked at his profile, wondering when it had happened. When had her baby boy turned into this man? Oh, she knew he had some growing up to do. Hell, so did she. But she'd looked at his profile, at the broad forehead that reminded her so much of his father, and his nose that was so like hers had been, and she'd been so struck by his beauty, tears had coursed down her face.

Noticing, he'd glanced at her self-consciously. "What's the matter?"

She got herself under control and gave him a wavering mother's smile. "God, you're gorgeous."

"All moms think that about their kids."

"Yeah." She sniffled again. But not all moms were right. She was right. "Are you ready to go home?" she'd asked.

"I thought I'd hang out on Dad's boat tonight. There's a kid my age whose family is renting a slip at the marina. I thought maybe we'd play some beach volleyball or something. I already asked Dad if it was okay. He told me to check with you."

Well. He'd been hers for a total of twenty-seven seconds. "Is your father going to be there?"

"Yeah."

"Was that a yes?" The man's voice in her ear startled Tori.

She drew back slightly. The Jude Law look-alike smiled, transporting her back to the club and reality.

She'd completely missed his approach. Pity. She would have enjoyed that.

"Uh," she said. *Good one, Tori.* Smiling provocatively, she tried again. "I'm afraid I was miles away. What was the question?"

"May I buy you a drink?"

Ooh. A man who said *may I.*

He had a nice voice, deep but not too deep. And that physique.

She picked up her margarita. "Maybe you could buy me the next one." Rising to her feet, she winked at Elaine, Nell and Pattie, then led the man away from the table where they could talk.

She could feel his eyes on her, checking her out the way she'd checked him out moments ago. She knew how she looked. Her black pants were tight but not too tight. They were slung low. Almost too low. And nothing said *look at me* more clearly than her red silk tank.

They settled in an area where they didn't

have to yell. They chatted for a while. She learned that his name was Adam. He was thirty-five and a doctor, no less. Didn't that beat all?

He said all the right things, leaning in just far enough to let her know he'd like to get closer. He was divorced.

"Yes, me, too."

And he had three sons.

"I have one."

"We live in Grand Haven. I don't usually bring my boat up to Charlevoix. I'm awfully glad I did."

True to his word, he bought her a drink. And she knew he was hers for the asking. Any second now he was going to offer himself up on a silver platter.

"What do people in Charlevoix do for fun?" he asked suggestively.

"The same as people from Grand Haven," she answered, just as suggestively.

He smiled.

And she said, "Could I ask you something, Adam?"

"Ask away."

"Do I make you drool?"

He wiped his mouth with the back of his hand.

For some reason, Tori glanced back at her table of friends before asking, "What do you see when you look at me?"

"Seriously?" he quipped.

She nodded, running her acrylic fingernail slowly up his forearm.

"I see beauty. Your hair. Your eyes. Your clothes. Your body. Perfection. You must know you're gorgeous. I like gorgeous. A lot."

Tori didn't know what was wrong with her. She'd heard it before. Tonight it failed to move her. Finally, she sighed. "Thank you for the drink."

"Where are you going?"

"Back to my friends."

She left him standing there, ripe for some other woman's taking.

Pattie, Nell and Elaine all stared at her as if she'd grown back her old nose. "What?" she asked.

"We didn't expect to see you again tonight," Pattie declared.

"Was something wrong with him?" Elaine asked.

"No, he was perfect."

"I don't understand," Nell said. "I thought you wanted perfection."

Tori made a face. What could she say? *Damn you, Caroline Moore?* She probably should have thanked Caroline for this new-found depth of character. Maybe she would.

In a hundred years. Maybe she wanted to be more than a body and a pretty face. Maybe she already was.

"You girls ready to get out of here?"

"I've been ready," Pattie complained. "Where are we going next?"

"Shopping."

"No store is open this time of night," Nell insisted.

"The Internet is open all night."

Tori saw the three other women exchange glances.

"What are we shopping for?" Nell asked gently.

"Shoes, of course."

"What do you think, Anna?" Caroline asked, cradling her baby. "Should we answer the door? Or should we pretend we're not home?"

Anna Maria Moore stared into her mother's eyes.

"You're right. We should answer the door. It's just that I can't seem to get enough of looking at you."

Anna pulled the most precious little face. And Caroline rose carefully to her feet. Checking first, she opened the door to a delivery man.

"Package for Caroline Moore," he said.

"Looks like you already have a package, and a tiny one at that."

Caroline was adjusting to the way people in small towns talked to everyone. If she happened to check her mailbox while the mailman was there, it could be half an hour before he stopped talking and went on to the rest of his route. It was the same way when she went to the fish market or the grocery or to the gas station. By the end of the visit, nobody was a stranger. She'd never seen this deliveryman before, but she returned his friendly smile.

"She's two weeks old today."

"Congratulations. The wife and I have four grandchildren. You think kids are great. Wait'll you get grandchildren. I need a signature." He pointed to a line on his clipboard.

She took the pen he offered and signed where he indicated, no easy feat with a baby in her arms. Caroline didn't mind.

Anna had only been home for two days. Although she was premature, she'd taken to her mother's breast like a little pro. Shane had been right that day in the hospital. The baby was strong. She was a fighter. And she liked to suck her little thumb. He was right about something else. Anna's hair was fine, wispy and red, her fingers dainty, her toes adorable.

Caroline had called Maria, her grandfather's former housekeeper to tell her about the baby. Maria had been thrilled with Caroline's choice of middle name. She'd also been happy to learn that little Anna didn't have a skinny neck and prominent Adam's apple. Like Andy had said, she hardly had any neck at all.

Andy and Shane. Shane and Andy. It was amazing how often she thought of them.

"Are you going to stand there holding that package all day?" Shane asked, coming into the room from the nursery where he'd been finishing putting together more baby items.

She stared at him, gaping. She'd been doing that all morning. She couldn't help it.

He took the baby from her, his hands nearly bigger than she was. Anna never seemed to mind all the jostling.

Caroline still made no move to open the lightweight box in her hand. She was too busy watching the silent exchange between Shane and her daughter. It was almost as if Caroline wasn't even here. She didn't have it in her to mind.

Shane was careful to support little Anna's head. She practically fit in one hand. He'd forgotten the sweet smell of newborns.

Somehow he'd forgotten how small they were and how their cries could jolt a grown man awake in the middle of the night.

She was an amazing baby. Of course, he may have been a tad biased. She slept a lot. But when she wasn't sleeping, she was extremely alert. She was studying him right now, feature by feature. It was the funniest thing. It was as if she thought she should know him from somewhere, but couldn't place him.

"Hi, there," he said, holding her so that they were at eye level. "I'm Shane."

He would look into those eyes thousands of times during the next fifty years. He would look into her mother's even more. He looked into Caroline's now. "Hi," he said.

She brought her hand up to his face. His bare face.

Caroline hadn't said anything when he'd arrived earlier, but he'd caught her looking at him much the way Anna had just looked at him, as if she knew him from somewhere but couldn't quite place him without his beard.

"What made you decide to shave?"

He'd been emotional for two weeks. In fact, he'd broken down and cried when Andy finally opened up about what had happened the day Brian drowned. His son had described the outing and the sun, and how Brian had taken off his life jacket to try to fish something out of the water. Neither of the boys had thought anything of it when Brian hung the life jacket on the mast to dry.

And then the wind came up, slamming into the sail, catching Brian on the side of his head. Andy had used his fist to knock on the boat's hull, mimicking the sound of the impact of metal and Brian's skull.

Shane had let his tears fall. "I miss him," he'd said. "I miss him every day, son. I guess we always will."

Andy had cried, too.

"It's a sad fact of life that we can't save everybody." For a long time, Shane had mourned his marriage. In a sense, he'd mourned it the way Andy mourned his best friend. "Maybe, somehow, the losses make the successes all the more poignant. Who knows why Brian died, and yet Caroline and Anna lived. Maybe there is no reason. Maybe it's enough that we love, that we bare our soul to someone who knows us, truly knows us."

It was during that revelation that Shane had decided to shave his beard. It had taken him another week to do it.

Caroline ran her hand along Shane's smooth cheek. "What made you decide to shave?" she asked again.

Clearing his throat, he said, "I figured you deserved to see me, all of me, if I was going to ask you to marry me."

"You figured that, did you?"

Shane felt a smile lurking. "I'm Shane Grady. I run the marina. I have a fifteen-year-old son who's going to be the death of me, a difficult ex-wife, a boat, a house, and not much else, but whatever I have, I'll share, because I've never been in love like this."

It was Caroline's turn to sniffle. "I'm Caroline Moore. And this is Anna. I have a law degree and a closet full of beautiful shoes, a few precarious friendships, and before I moved here, I'd never been in love at all."

She couldn't stop looking at his face. It was completely different without the beard. He had an angular jaw and a wide mouth. A poet's mouth. She couldn't decide if he looked older or younger. She liked him exactly as he was.

Remembering the package, she shook it lightly. Nothing rattled. "Shall I open it?"

He carried the baby, she the package, into the kitchen where she took a knife from the drawer and sliced through the packaging tape. She lifted the lid easily enough, but had to remove several layers of packaging foam in order to reach what was inside.

She drew in a loud breath, her mouth forming a large *O*.

"Aren't they a little big for Anna?" Shane asked.

Caroline lifted a beautiful pair of baby shoes from the box. She turned them over, looking at them from every angle. "They're made by hand in a little village on the coast of Italy."

"Who're they from?" Shane rummaged through the rest of the packaging foam.

Caroline wasn't surprised he didn't find a card. She knew who they were from. "They're from Tori."

"Why would she go to so much trouble?"

"Remember when I asked her if she was giving us her permission? I believe she's given us something better. She's giving us her blessing."

Even baby Anna responded to the wonder in Caroline's voice.

"That's nice," Shane said quietly. "Does this mean you will?"

"Will?" Once again, Caroline found herself looking at the stranger before her. "Oh, you mean will I marry you?"

"That is the question on the table."

She rolled her eyes, but in the end she smiled. "Yes."

"Yes?"

"Yes, I'll marry you."

He leaned down and kissed her mouth gently, Anna between them. When it ended, Caroline found herself looking at his hands.

They were big hands, working hands, capable hands, nurturing hands. They held her daughter, who barely weighed five pounds. If necessary, she knew he would carry the weight of the world for them both.

Bringing the tip of her finger to her throat, Caroline traced the charm that had been her mother's. She thought about her mother, and how much she'd missed. She thought about her grandmother, Anna, too, and how much she'd been loved.

It was mind-boggling, really, the way things had turned out. History didn't repeat itself, exactly, but similar situations had a way of circling around, generation by generation. It had begun right here in Harbor Woods more than sixty years ago when two boys had climbed a water tower, and later had fallen in love with the same girl.

And here Caroline was, gazing lovingly at her own precious baby girl, the seed planted by one man, to be raised by another. Caroline would pass along all the stories to little Anna, so she would know her ancestors.

She and Shane had many decisions to make. The house in Lake Forest was on the market, as was Karl's house on Prospect Street. She and Shane would have to decide where they would live. Karl had left the lighthouse property to Shane. Perhaps they would live there. She wanted Andy to be a part of that decision. They had a wedding to plan. It would be Caroline's first. She hadn't yet worn the silk dress she'd purchased the day she'd met Tori. Suddenly, Caroline knew the perfect occasion for it. Shane would probably ask Andy to be his best man. Caroline would need a witness, too. She had a candidate in mind.

Tomorrow she would thank Tori for the baby shoes. Soon, they would be more than unlikely friends. Caroline would be Shane's wife and Andy's stepmother. That would make Caroline and Tori practically family. She could hardly wait to hear what Tori had to say about that.

ABOUT THE AUTHOR

Sandra Steffen has always been a story-teller. She began nurturing this hidden talent by concocting adventures for her brothers and sisters, even though the boys were more interested in her ability to hit a baseball over the barn — an automatic home run. She didn't begin her pursuit of publication until she was a young wife and mother of four sons. Since her thrilling debut as a published author in 1992, thirty-three of her novels have graced bookshelves across the country.

Professional reviewers have called Sandra a veritable master at creating characters, and her books well written, satisfying and intelligent. Her most cherished review came from her youngest son recently when he said, "Mom, I hear your voice as I'm reading your book."

This winner of the RITA® Award, the W.I.S.H. Award and the National Readers'

Choice Award enjoys traveling with her husband. Usually their destinations are settings for her upcoming books. They are empty nesters these days. Who knew it could be so much fun? Please visit her at www.sandrasteffen.com.